"I should have gone with Manuel to England and faced up to your father," June said. "Now it's too late. You've wanted to find me, but now that you have, you can't forgive."

"I don't hate you," Claire told her mother. "It's just that our relationship seems doomed. I'm sure you know what I mean. Ricardo will have told you."

June smiled indulgently. "That he loves you? My dear, how long have you known Ricardo? A few days? A few days in a new, glamorous place. A handsome young man with a fast car. And for him, a pretty, pale English girl." She put a hand over Claire's. "Of course it's enough to turn the heads of both of you. Of course it's totally understandable. But it's not a good enough reason for ruining the lives of other people," she pointed out soberly. "It really is not. One day you'll wake up and find yourself out of love with this handsome, and may I say very willful young man, and you'll simply float off back home, but there'll be no turning back for the others. The damage will have been done."

"Did anyone say that to you," Claire retorted, "when you fell in love with Manuel while on vacation and ran away from me and my father?"

Coming soon—two more enchanting romances by Vicky Maxwell:

CHOSEN CHILD
FLIGHT TO THE VILLA MISTRA

the Other Side of Summer

VICKY MAXWELL

ace books

A Division of Charter Communications Inc.
A GROSSET & DUNLAP COMPANY
360 Park Avenue South
New York, New York 10010

THE OTHER SIDE OF SUMMER

Copyright © 1977 by Vicky Maxwell

An ACE Book

First Ace printing: February 1979

Published simultaneously in Canada

Printed in U.S.A.

the Other Side of Summer

ONE

All photographs of the errant runaway had been destroyed when the divorce went through, but people who had known her said Claire's mother was tall, about the same height as her daughter, with soft blonde hair like hers and an oval face, with the same gray eyes. "She did not have the sort of skin to withstand heat." Aunt Marcia's flaring rancor indicated that nineteen years had not been enough time for forgiveness. "I wouldn't be surprised if she was wrinkled like a prune by now. Even Spanish women who are genetically accustomed to the dry air and hot sun age early. I'd be surprised to hear June had any looks left, especially since she has probably had to work hard. That fellow Manuel what's-'is-name, that she ran off with, was as poor as a church mouse. He was only twenty at the time and his father had died so he had to support his mother and a whole lot of younger sisters and brothers. Your mother," she added disapprovingly, inferring that age brings sobriety, "was twenty-five."

They were sitting at a tea table in the garden of the Davisons' house in a Surrey village where Claire had, inevitably, spent a great deal of her time. It was spring and the daffodils streamed in golden glory down the length of the long garden. Forsythia raised its spiky branches all along the board fence and the sky was a magnificent shade of sapphire blue. The resemblance between Marcia Davison and Claire's late father was uncanny. Tall, with angular proportions, she wore her graying hair in a careless knot at the base of her neck. At forty-five her skin was flawless and virtually unlined. One could see, in that curious way that defies analysis, that Nancy her daughter had her looks from Marcia, though Nancy had the neat features that her mother lacked, small frail bones and a soft, kittenish style. Nancy, Claire always thought, was a secret girl. After knowing her all her life, loving her, she could not have given anyone a character analysis of her cousin. She was three years older than Claire and enormously self-assured. Her hair was the color her mother's had been twenty years before, a rich auburn. She wore it cut short in a sophisticated and trendy style with a fringe curling on her forehead and her small ears peeping through. She had almond-shaped green eyes and darkly penciled brows. Aunt Marcia said as Nancy came in: "Claire is thinking of going to Spain to look for her mother."

The silence in the room was intense. Nancy's eyes met those of her mother and Claire said mildly: "So? Is there something I ought to know?"

There had been a touch of guilt in that swift glance.

"I think—" Nancy began.

Claire cut her off, not rudely but because she did not want her cousin to say anything that might weaken her resolve or shake her nerve. "I am doing this on my own, and I am determined to go ahead with it. I have a right to know my mother, regardless of what she has done." She added defensively: "Out of sheer curiosity, I would like to hear her side of the story. Maybe my mother fell so madly and crazily in love that she couldn't do anything about it."

"I am sure she did," snapped her aunt. "I've never doubted that. Why else, for she had nothing to go to? As I said, the man was a pauper."

"Is that so reprehensible? People have been running off with ineligible young men since the beginning of time." Claire managed a half-hearted smile.

"I don't think there are many women who would leave a two-year-old baby," replied Nancy critically. "Your mother must have been incredibly unfeeling to leave you, Claire. You, above all people, must recognize that."

"If she was so incredibly unfeeling, would she have fallen passionately in love?" How strange, Claire thought, that I the bereft, should be defending the runaway. Nancy had flopped into a wicker chair and was gazing up into the shady branches of an apple tree. Her aunt was looking at her nails. Claire gave them a little more time. When it became clear there was to be no sympathetic meeting point, she added: "It may seem odd, Aunt Marcia, but I've never actually known.

How did my mother meet this Spaniard?" Marcia looked up with a surprised expression and Claire added mildly: "Children know instinctively when a question is taboo." As she grew up the subject had been tucked into a secret recess of her mind. Since her father's death, when her aloneness had taken on larger proportions, it had begun to fester a little.

Marcia said: "She met him when John was working on that bridge in Scotland. They left you with me, so your mother had a lot of time on her hands. When she returned, Manzales came after her."

"Was Manzales an engineer too?"

"An engineer? I shouldn't think so. If I remember rightly he was based in London. What do Spaniards do here?" Marcia asked patronizingly. "It's Greeks who go in for restaurants, isn't it? I've no idea. I expect he was just loafing around. Anyway, your father finished the job and came back to find June in a stew. As you can imagine, there was a high old rumpus. Then, before anything could be sorted out, Manzales got word that his father had died and he rushed off back to Spain because he said he would have to support this vast family. Your mother, all in a moment, had a brainstorm and took off with him—without even a toothbrush. So you can see it was not exactly a rosy future June had to look forward to," she added, leaning forward and looking concentratedly into Claire's eyes as though the fact had to be rammed home. "I really hate to think what she found when she arrived."

"Didn't you ever write?"

Marcia replied, tight-lipped: "I didn't write. I

was not too pleased with her, as you might imagine."

"Meaning you had to take some of the responsibility for me?"

Her aunt flushed. "You know what I mean. John was my brother and your mother let him down badly. Where do you expect I felt my loyalty lay?"

"I'm sorry I said that, Aunt Marcia." Claire had been edgy since deciding on this plan. Easily upset by the things people said, in spite of the fact that she had asked the questions and demanded straight answers.

"That's all right, dear," her aunt replied kindly, consciously relaxing now that the ill-feeling, so long dammed up, had been released. "You've had a bad time these past eighteen months. None of us are really ourselves." Riddled with guilt, she meant, because they were all glad to see Claire's father dead, for no one could wish a man who was suffering so to go on living.

Nancy said in that infuriatingly superior voice she was inclined to use with her younger cousin: "You obviously don't want advice. I don't know what sort of relationship you can start up after twenty years with a mother who—" At a warning look from her mother, Nancy broke off.

"I have no reason to believe my mother doesn't want to see me," Claire said, "if that was what you were going to say. I was removed, wasn't I, after the court case?" Her father had taken a job in Canada and Claire had gone along with a nanny. They had come home when Claire was six. "After all," she added, "my mother has been in touch. Aunt Marcia," she said sharply, "that is the second time you and Nancy have exchanged glances. What have you been hiding?"

"Twice?" echoed Marcia, looking uncomfortable. "I knew about one. When you were fifteen."

"I had another letter when I was twelve," Claire told them, confessing at last. "I kept it to myself. I knew instinctively it would cause trouble." This first one had been a nice, kind letter not calculated to pull at a child's emotions. Virtually, what it said was: *We're here if you want us*. And the one that came three years later! Claire would never forget, nor wish to experience again the storm, the bitterness, the recriminations that followed. "I suppose Father wrote and told her not to do it again, because I didn't hear any more. What are you two holding back?" she asked now.

Nancy said: "Look here, Claire, you mustn't blame us. We had to do what Uncle John asked us to do. After all, he had custody."

"Of course, I understand." Claire knew about the court case. John Richardson had told the lawyers and the court that his wife had run off with a penniless Spanish rascal and God knew what her future would be. At least he had been able, with the help of a right-thinking English judge, to hold onto the child. For a long time Claire had felt vaguely grateful that she had been saved from some unknown and unnamed horror. Now, at twenty-one, she was not only able to see that her father had not by any means been an easy man, but she could assess her own loss.

"So what have you been hiding?"

"Nothing, really. But perhaps you ought to know that before the letter came—the one we knew about—a man—a Spaniard—turned up at school asking to see you." Claire, when she was old enough, had been sent to the same boarding school as Nancy so that her cousin could keep an eye on the younger girl. "Of course you know the staff had been warned that you were not to see any Spaniards."

"I didn't know. Father left no stone unturned, did he?" Claire asked, smarting.

"He only had your interests at heart," her aunt pointed out. "He didn't think it was right for a child to be torn in two directions."

Claire swallowed her anger. "Who was this Spaniard?"

"He said he was your mother's brother-in-law. He wanted to see you, but—" Green eyes met gray and Claire felt the frustration of years rising to a peak. As though she felt her cousin's antagonism, Nancy looked uncomfortable. "Miss Olliphant called me in because she couldn't get Uncle John on the telephone."

"And you, not yet eighteen, told the man he was not allowed to see me!" Claire was outraged. "How dared you? How dared you presume to make decisions in my life?"

"Claire, dear, it was for your own good," exclaimed Aunt Marcia, looking distressed.

"Was it? Nancy could decide that?" Claire flashed. "Well, Aunt Marcia, Nancy had no right. And now I realize that our headmistress, at least, had a heart. If she had not felt it was right for me to meet that man she would have sent him off with a flea in his ear according to instructions. Instead, she tried to get in touch with Father. That could only have been because she thought I ought to know my mother's people."

Nancy tossed her head. "I was more or less responsible for you" she said. "You came to my school to be with me. Uncle John wanted you to have some family with you. Whatever you say, I did have some responsibility."

"So you saw this man!" Claire was keeping her anger under control. "Perhaps you will tell me what he was like? What was his name?"

Nancy said: "Ollie introduced him only as Señor Manzales. He was tall and dark."

"He might really have been my stepfather. How old was he?"

"No, he wasn't your stepfather. He would have been about twenty-one, I should think, at the time. He was very good-looking. Your mother's husband was supposed to be very handsome too."

"Yes." She had always known that. A woman did not leave a husband and a child for a drab little man. "I think you might have let him see me," Claire said, still angry. "It would not have hurt anyone. He could have told my mother what I looked like, at any rate."

"As a matter of fact, he did—see you, I mean. By chance, your class walked past the windows as we were standing in Ollie's study. I pointed you out."

"Did you?" Claire brightened. "What did he say?"

"He said. 'She looks like Juanita.'"

Juanita! She had a queer sort of shock, as though the image of her mother had receded, claimed by a foreign land.

"I wish you weren't so angry, Claire. I did what seemed best. What your father wanted."

Claire turned frustratedly to her aunt. "I don't see that anyone could have done anything else," Marcia said.

At least her mother had wanted to know her, and perhaps she still did. The visit of Manuel's brother must have come in reply to the protest her father would have sent when he discovered Claire received a letter from Spain. June had redoubled her efforts to get in touch. The knowledge gave Claire a certain confidence. She said: "I have this money from the house. I want to know if my mother needs help now that I am in a position to help her."

Nancy looked startled. Marcia gasped, but when she spoke her words came carefully. "It's inevitable that such a lot of money should burn a hole in your pocket, dear. It's natural, for a girl who has never had much to spend. But although it probably seems a fortune to you, it's not much more than the price of a house. And you are going to need a house of your own."

Claire laughed. "At my age?"

"One day. You haven't had the most enviable childhood," Aunt Marcia said kindly, looking desperately worried. "You deserve the money, dear. And the last year, though you were so brave about it, was certainly hell for you."

It had been hell it was true, but that was over now. The doctor said it was not unknown for people with a terminal illness to turn against those who had cared for them and loved them. It was just another of life's tragedies that people did not always go out of it leaving happy memories.

Suddenly Marcia capitulated. "Of course you

must see your mother, simply because she is your mother, but how about taking Nancy along with you? Heaven alone knows what you're going to find and—" she broke off for Claire had risen from the cane chair. She stood looking out over the daffodils with her long pale hair lifting on a little breeze. She looked so extraordinarily like June at this age that Marcia experienced a shock. June, who had been so flighty, so impetuous, so generous and so heartbreakingly foolish. She said in a panicky voice: "You and Nancy will go together. We will fix it up. And please, Claire, think again. Don't do anything hasty. Your mother abandoned you. Life is ridiculous at times, I know, but don't let it be as ridiculous as that. What money you have is yours. Your father wanted you to have it. What on earth has your mother done to des——"

Claire had turned and was looking at her aunt. "I am going by myself," she said, breaking in politely but firmly. "And I will do what I like with what is mine. There has been enough interference, kindly though I am sure it was meant."

"No, dear. You mustn't go like that."

"No, Claire, really, I'll come with you!" Nancy exclaimed.

Claire began to walk across the lawn towards the side door. She did not want to argue. She was going to Spain, and she was going alone. Nothing, and nobody, was going to alter that.

TWO

Anyone with any sense, Claire said to herself as she flew over the foam-edged Atlantic where it touched the Brittany coast and swept down across the rugged, snow-capped mountains of northern Spain, would have written first. She could not have said why she had not done so, unless it was the fear of being turned down or the equal fear of finding something she could not face. In nineteen years had June Richardson—or Juanita Manzales as her name was now— become so totally Spanish that there would be no meeting point with her discarded English daughter? Would guilt stand in the way? Resentment on Claire's part?

She came out of her dream to hear the voice on the intercom saying: "You will be landing at Malaga airport in approximately forty minutes. The temperature there is seventy degrees."

And that will suit me very well, Claire said to herself, remembering the cold wind she had left behind in England. She looked out of the window on to gray-green mountains directly below and in the distance, red earth glowing up between rows of green crops. She had expected the land to be more barren. She had been astonished at the greenness of the central plains. *Dried-up land and women wrinkled like prunes*, Aunt Marcia's voice sounded in her ears. Well, it seemed she might be wrong, at least in spring, about the first pronouncement. Perhaps she might be wrong about other things. Claire felt a little rush of excitement, an emotional jump towards happiness that nearly took her breath away. This could be the most wonderful summer of her life. A summer towards which she had been moving imperceptibly since she came of age.

Claire had arranged for a Hertz car to be waiting at the airport. She was accustomed, since visiting America with her father on his last job, to driving on the right hand side of the road. She put her one suitcase on the back seat and took out the road map the Spanish Tourist Bureau had provided. She had a good sense of direction. "It will not be difficult," said the Hertz man. "The road signs are good."

She asked him how long it would take her to drive to the place where June lived. "I do not know. Tell me, what is the nearest town?"

She showed him the cross marked by the helpful man at the bureau. "Ah! An hour, I think. Or perhaps a little more. First, you must go into Malaga, and from there it will take about an hour.

The road follows the coast. It is a very beautiful drive."

It was indeed a beautiful drive. The road hugged the mountains and the mountains hugged the sea. Claire drove slowly until she became used to the car, but once free of the town she put on speed, whirling round hairpin bends where the road cut into the rugged, tree clad, often almost perpendicular hillsides, speeding across little stone-built bridges that straddled the head of a narrow valley, dipping down into a bay choked with rocks and white with foam, then speeding out of it and up again on a long climb that led to the top of a ridge. Several times she pulled in at roadside clearings and climbed out to look back at the view, mile upon mile of folded hills, here scrub-covered, there bush-clad, and often gaunt, spectacular, overwhelmingly bleak where great rocks burst out of the earth and seemed to hang, threateningly, in midair. As she went north the mountains became more rugged, the views more spectacular. It was what she needed to take her mind off the immediate future.

At two o'clock she stopped at a little restaurant perched on an outcrop of rock at the roadside. There were no tourists here, only half a dozen Spaniards lounging at the bar drinking apéritifs from tiny glasses; one old man, his hat down on his eyes, dozed over coffee at a table on the concrete forecourt. Claire ordered a coffee for herself. The men stared at her, their black eyes curious. She carried her cup and saucer outside. Now, in the silence, she could hear the thunder of the waves breaking against the rocks far below.

Out at sea the water was calm enough but there must have been some breeze for two yachts were sweeping northwards at a fair rate towards Barcelona. Nearer at hand a lone fishing-boat lay at anchor.

She finished her drink and unwilling to face again the curious eyes of the men at the bar, left the cup on a table outside. Consulting the map, she decided the village could be another ten kilometers ahead. She climbed into the car and set off again. Here trees and cactus gave way to rocks. It was easy to believe that the people would be poor and certainly there were no signs of tourism. Except for the magnificent, vast, black-silhouetted bull that leaped up on an occasional skyline to astonish her, there were no advertisements. The villages in the valleys were sunbaked and poor looking, the people scruffy, the children at the roadside ill-clad. She passed few cars. Half an hour later she swept up a long, winding hill and turning the corner looked down into a wide bay. At the far side a small town huddled and on the opposite hill there were several complexes of new houses. Claire pulled in at a look-out and consulted her map. This town could be her destination. Yes, the map confirmed it.

She climbed out of the car and stood on the edge of a precipitous drop looking out over the bay, wondering what to do. In Spanish villages, the Tourist Bureau had told her, everyone knew everyone else. It was unlikely that she would have much trouble finding the Manzales. This triangular-shaped collection of apricot-colored roofs hugging the sea was scarcely a village. Now she felt a brush of apprehension. What was she going to do? Book into a hotel—if hotel there was—and write a letter to her mother? Telephone? (If they had a telephone.) With only a box number to start with, if she could not locate the family she would have to write a letter anyway, and then wait. She climbed back into the car. Her fingers trembled as she touched the ignition switch, then feeling extremely nervous, she ran the car down into the little bay.

The town was tightly packed together. Turning in off the road, Claire found herself facing a row of newish shops. She drove past them and followed a narrow, twisting little lane closely hemmed in by white stucco houses with sloping tiled roofs until she found herself in a small square. There were palm trees fringing the pavement and in the center, an enormous church. There were a dozen or more vehicles parked against the footpath. She parked the car and took a path that was little more than an alleyway but which appeared to lead towards the beach. She had already made up her mind to ask someone in a shop or public building, but clearly she would have to wait until four o'clock, for the Spanish Tourist Board had warned her that between the hours of two and four Spain slept.

This was clearly the old part of the town for quaint, picturesque buildings leaned higgledy-piggledy one against another with tiny fences in front. Gardens not more than a few square feet in size were jammed with luxuriant flowering plants. Bougainvillaea, red, purple, pink and white climbed up every wall and hung down from the eaves. The shops were closed.

And then she saw a bar. A large bar it was, and

modern. She stood in the doorway looking in. There was a glass box at the end of the counter stacked with hard boiled eggs, lobsters, long bread rolls. She had not felt hungry before, but now suddenly it seemed easier to eat than to face up to asking questions that might precipitate a meeting before she was ready for it. The barman came forward. *"Buenos dias."*

She said haltingly: "I don't speak Spanish."

"Then 'good afternoon,' " he replied, smiling. "You are a visitor?"

"Yes."

"What would you like? A drink? Some lunch?"

"Yes, both, thank you." It was a relief to talk. The journey with only her own thoughts for company had been too long. "Some local wine, please."

He poured out a glassful. "You would like to choose something from here?" He indicated the array of delicious looking food inside the glass counter. She asked for a lobster salad. The barman was friendly and courteous. He came round to her side and drew up a stool for her to sit on. "You are staying here in the town?"

"For a few days."

"You have friends?"

"I may look up some people," she replied cautiously. "I don't suppose you know anyone called Manzales?"

"Manuel Manzales?" The man's dark eyebrows shot up and he smiled broadly. "Ah yes, I do know Manuel Manzales. Everyone knows Manuel Manzales. But he does not live in the town. He lives up on a hill further back towards Malaga. You would like to telephone? You can call from here," he said. His eyes were alight with pleasure now that he had placed her and assumed they shared a friend.

Claire caught her breath. Her face was suddenly aflame. Reasonably sophisticated as she was, she could not have said what made her react so. I am more hung up over this thing than I realized, she thought, trying hard to meet the man's puzzled eyes. The barman was perceptive. "You want to know where is the house? You want to call and surprise them? No?"

"No," Claire replied. "I don't want to do that. Besides, it is the siesta time and I would not want to disturb them now."

The barman chuckled. "Manuel Manzales does not have the siesta. He is only out of bed about the middle of the day, and then he stay up until three, maybe four next morning. He does not need the siesta."

"His wife may rest."

"His wife is English." The man's eyes danced. "You are English. You know they do not have the siesta." Suddenly he blinked, gave her a hard look, then said curiously: "You are related to Señora Manzales? She looks like you."

"I expect all English people look rather alike to a Spaniard," Claire said, finishing her wine at one gulp. "Most of us are fair." But he was not taken in. She saw it in his face when she had to look up. For a giddy moment she was tempted to ask the barman about the family and then he turned away to collect her salad and she was saved from herself. He put the plate down before her, refilled her wine glass, then went off through a door leaving her alone.

So they lived here, June Manzales her mother, and that man who had run off with her. Claire had not expected the search to be so effortless. She wished she could think of a tactful question to ask the barman that would give her some clue as to the Manzales' situation. How they lived. What Manuel did. She felt a need to be warned.

The barman returned. "What does Señor Manzales do?"

"Ah!" replied the Spaniard. "He is a very big man. A very important man in the town. He is what you call a property developer."

"A *what!*"

The barman, sensing something amiss, leaned his folded arms on the bar and thrust his dark face concernedly forward. "I will fill your glass, Señorita?"

She shook her head. Inexplicably, she would have liked to put her forehead down on her arms and cry.

"I will telephone Señor Manzales for you? He could come to get you. You will wait here while he come for you?"

She shook her head again. "I will have another drink, after all, thank you."

He refilled her glass. She drank the wine slowly, in tiny sips. The man leaned back against his shelves, watching her thoughtfully. After a while he went through the door. Had she been deliberately misinformed? Was the tale of insuperable foreign poverty a ruse to keep her mother and herself apart? No, the family knew her better than that. Claire considered the situation in its new light. So, June Manzales was well off, well cared for, a member of a family of substance. Why had she not written? Why had she not come to England to visit her daughter? Since Claire turned eighteen she had been free of the court's jurisdiction. Could she assume, then, that her mother had forgotten about her? Could the family have been right, that June Manzales was selfish, casual and down-right unkind? Claire sat forlornly on her bar stool, feeling lost.

Nobody came in. By the time Claire had finished her drink she had still not come to a decision. They will think I came to them because Father died. They will ask me why I did not come before, she suddenly realized. It is three years since I, too, have been free to make the approaches. But her mother had said, in both those letters, that they wanted her to know they were here if she needed them. I must readjust my thoughts. Get into a different channel. They don't need my help, and I don't need theirs. There was a gap now where there had not been one before and she did not know how to close it.

THREE

Claire climbed down from her stool and knocked loudly on the bar. The empty room with its potted palms, its wrought iron gee-gaws, its little tables and chairs, could be attractive and gay in the evening. Now in its afternoon shadow it looked like an overdressed lady with nowhere to go. The barman swung through the door leaving it to slam behind him. "You have finish?" Two magnificent gold teeth gleamed. "You will have another glass of *vino?*"

"No, thank you."

"Ah-h-h!" He made a face, cajoling. "On the house, as the English say."

She smiled. "That's very kind, but no, I have to drive a car. I have had enough. How much do I owe you?"

"Ah!" the man said as though she had raised a tremendous point of interest. He placed his hands

21

on his hips and settled back on his heels as though about to embark on a long discussion. "So you have your own car, and did not need Señor Manzales to collect you? I did not know. Ah-h—! I see!"

She thought he must be lonely and wanting her company, but she needed to get away to think. "I would like to pay my bill, " she said.

"You will go to see the Manzales in your own car? I will tell you how to find the villa. It is not easy. It will take you ten minutes, maybe twenty. That is," he shrugged amusingly, "if you do not get lost."

She began to be irritated by his garrulousness. "Please tell me what I owe you."

"Ah! You owe." With a flamboyant gesture the little Spaniard picked up a pencil in one hand and a pad in another. "Let me see. *Langosta. Ensalada. Pan. Dos vinos.*" He wrote the bill out slowly, laboriously, then stared at it, frowning. Impatient now that it seemed he was holding her up deliberately, Claire put some notes down on the bar. "One hundred eighty pesetas," he said at last with a triumphant flourish of his pen. He picked up the notes and counted them slowly, then paused to look at her again. "You will see the town before you go?"

"Yes."

"The beach is nice."

She held out her hand for the change and reluctantly he gave it to her. "*Adios.*"

She climbed down from her stool and turned towards the exit. "Good-bye." The sun had moved a little farther down in the sky and the crushed white buildings with their sunshine-

colored tiles cast black shadows in the lanes.
Claire wandered back to the car, feeling depressed
and still faintly irritated by the barman's inexplicable behavior. She unlocked the door and slipped
into the driving seat, rolled down the window and
rested an elbow on the top of the glass. What to
do? She allowed her mind to go blank, staring in
front of her at a creeper-clad wall, scarcely seeing
it. Staring. A tall young man in jeans and T-shirt
came swinging through the opening from the lane
that led to the bar. She watched him without
interest. He stood looking round as though searching for someone. Claire pressed the ignition
switch and the engine sprang to life. The young
man turned sharply, looking her way, then he ran
across the intervening space directly towards the
car. He was devastatingly handsome. His gleaming black hair rolled back from a broad forehead in
luxuriant waves, and he was taller than the aver-
age Spaniard, finely built but with a look of
strength. He came right up to the car, placed a
brown hand on the door and bent down to look in.
His eyes were an incredible blue framed with the
thickest lashes Claire ever remembered.

He said: "Claire Richardson." It was not a question, and yet there was a query in those expressive
blue eyes.

"Yes," she said, her mind blank with surprise,
not wanting to guess who he could be. Not her
stepfather, for he was far too young.

The man nodded, satisfied, then ran around the
front of the car. The passenger door was locked.
Still with her mind blank, Claire leaned across and
slid the catch. She was aware of a feeling of being
lifted above her problems. She had a strange sen-

sation of sliding through to her destiny. The man jumped into the passenger seat, then held out his right hand. "I am Ricardo Manzales," he said. "Luiz called me. I live here, in the town. Just out of this square." He watched her face, examining it carefully. "You've changed," he said at last smiling.

She gasped, then cried delightedly, "It was you who came to St. Catherine's six years ago!"

"Yes. I, Ricardo Manzales. I can't tell you how happy Juanita was that I was able to see—well, even to glimpse you. They didn't tell me you were coming. But you will need a guide, anyway. The house is not so easy for a stranger to find. Would you like me to drive?"

Claire slid out of the driving seat and stood up. The sun beat down on her face. She put a hand over her eyes and waited for the sudden pounding of her heart to stop. When she looked up Ricardo was standing beside her. "What is the matter, Claire?" he asked, gently.

"Do you mind—I—I don't think I can face it, quite like that. I am sorry. I hope you'll understand. I—this is rather an ordeal for me. Did that man call you? The man in the bar."

"Yes; Luiz."

She gave a nervous little laugh. "I had a feeling he was holding me up. I didn't know why. Are all Spaniards so interfering or—does everyone know about me?"

He shrugged. "A little of both, perhaps. The Manzales are well known in the town. Well respected. And of course everyone knows Juanita had to leave her beloved daughter in England.

They always hope you will come. The family is very important in Spain."

"Your family?" She was startled once more.

He smiled. "Every family."

"Oh."

He took the keys gently from her fingers and locked the car doors. Sliding an arm through hers, he led her across the square and down a little lane. "There is a restaurant on the beach. We will talk there."

"Let's walk."

"No, no, that is not necessary. We will have a drink and talk at Eugenios." It was her first intimation that important Spanish affairs are conducted in bars and restaurants.

The shops and soaring balconies enclosed them as they made their way through the tiny town and out on to the end of the beach. Ricardo took her down some stone steps and then they walked together in silence to where a dozen tables and chairs stood beneath a rush canopy. One of the white-coated waiters came forward and shook Ricardo by the hand, bowed to Claire then led them to a small wooden table on the outer edge.

"What will you have, Claire?"

She had really drunk all she wanted that day but she asked for wine. Ricardo sat down opposite. He smiled at her again delightedly. "So," he said softly. "You have come at last."

It was the way he said it that touched her, as though all these years the family had waited for her. She felt a lump in her throat. "I—I want to talk about—"

"Juanita?"

"You call her that?" Claire felt faintly bruised by this sudden realization of how far her English mother had moved away. She subdued the confusion within her by telling herself it seemed pretentious for an Englishwoman to be called by a Spanish name.

He nodded.

"I cannot say 'Mother.' "

"Because she has not been a mother to you? She has not," Ricardo acceded without waiting for a reply, "but that is not her fault. The courts would not allow her to have you. It is hard to understand that anyone would want to part a baby from her mother. And when Juanita wrote to you she never got a reply. Only once, from your father." He raised his head, closed his eyes and put his fists to his forehead. "It was a very angry letter. And so when I was in England at the university Juanita sent me to your school, but I was not allowed to see you. Just a glimpse, and that is why I recognized you now."

Claire said: "I only received two letters."

"She wrote to you often. But," Ricardo pointed out reproachfully, "you did not answer even those two you received."

She said: "No, I didn't," and suddenly she saw that omission as an enormous crime. "The first one came when I was twelve. I hid it because I sensed there would be trouble if I showed it to my father. I suppose I was afraid to answer it." As a child Claire would have sensed that sending a reply would be siding with the enemy. She said carefully, keeping the resentment out of her voice: "If you were at a university in England, you had plenty of time to visit us."

"I took my instructions from Juanita. Your father had custody of you. She accepted that, but not easily. It had to be accepted. She wrote, but she did not try to get you out here. She and Manuel decided, because of your father's attitude, that you must be left to grow up in peace. That there was to be no tug-of-war between the parents. Did you not realize?"

"A child doesn't know these things. Has she—has she any children of her own? I mean, have Manuel and June had children?"

"Two boys. Juan is fourteen and Vicente eight."

"Oh."

"They are lovely boys," said Ricardo with pride, almost as though they were his own.

The waiter came with a bottle of wine and two glasses. They sat in silence until he went away. Then Ricardo said: "Juanita did not forget you because she had two new children." He had enormous sensitivity for a young man, as well as tremendous *élan*. "What I have often wondered," he added as he filled the glasses, "is why you did not come here when you were eighteen. You were surely free at eighteen to do as you liked?"

"Yes. That was when I left school. My father was an engineer, you know. He accepted a job in Canada, and took me with him."

Ricardo said dryly: "I do not want to be rude about your father, of course. But was that accidentally, or by design? He took you away also after the divorce."

Claire had always tried not to judge or criticize her father. It had clearly been a traumatic experience, this losing his young wife to a foreigner. "I was happy to go to Canada," she said evasively. "I had a wonderful time."

"You stayed there for three years, until now?"

"No. About eighteen months. Then my father's health began to fail and we returned to England. He was very ill. It was a bad time to show disloyalty."

"Disloyalty?" Ricardo looked quizzical.

"That is how he would have seen my visit to Spain. Of course he was bitter, dreadfully bitter, but he did love me very dearly, and I was all he had."

"He never thought of marrying again?"

"Yes, he did. There was a nice woman who would have suited him very well." Claire remembered how the explosion that had come out of her emotional admission of receiving June's letter had frightened Stephanie away.

"What happened?"

"She said my father was too tied up with bitterness from the past to put proper heart into a new marriage."

"That is sad."

"Yes. And you can see, I felt I was partly to blame."

"No," said Ricardo firmly. "No." He crashed his fist down on the tiny table so that the wine bottle wobbled dangerously and people next door looked up with interest. "Too often," said Ricardo with such excessive feeling, that she looked at him in surprise, "one has to carry the blame for something other people have done. You must not think of that again, Claire. If a man grows bitter over his problems, then it is because there is something in him that will not allow him to forget and forgive. In *him*," Ricardo repeated with emphasis and this time he thumped the table a little more softly. "And does your father know that you have come here now?"

"I should have said, he died. He was ill for eighteen months and then he died." Because she did not want to talk about that, or even receive sympathy, she rushed on: "I always meant to come and look for my mother some time. I suppose, if I had realized, I could have gone off when I was eighteen, but I never had enough money to finance such a trip, and of course I couldn't ask Father, or anyone else, for that matter. Anyway, one has to be older than that to set out alone to find someone in a strange country where one doesn't speak the language. It's not as though I was obsessed with the idea of finding her. I was a bit scared, to tell the truth. I thought it was probably something I couldn't cope with, and I thought how awful it would be if I did write and say I would like to see her but didn't have the money, and she should somehow raise my fare and then there would be trouble with Father, and I wouldn't be able to get back, and goodness knows what sort of untenable . . . ?" she trailed off to a stop.

Ricardo said gently: "I am sorry. I did not realize your father had died. Juanita does not know. Now, when she knows what has happened since you were of age she will understand. Shall I take you now to see her?"

"Please—first will you tell me something about her life. About the family. The man in the bar—

Luiz—said your brother is a very important man hereabouts, but my family told me he was very poor."

"Ah yes, the Manzales have always been poor," said Ricardo.

She suppressed a little smile saying dryly: "Do the poor people of Spain send their sons to England to be educated?"

He chuckled. "Yes, there are degrees of poverty. We have all been to foreign countries to 'finish.' Leopoldo to Germany, Teresa to France and Germany as an *au pair*, Leonora and Julia who are married now, to England. But your family was right if they said Manuel was poor when Juanita came. Spain was a very poor country, then. My grandfather had a great deal of land but it was not worth anything. Wherever you look you will see my grandfather's land," said Ricardo. "Stones and rocks and hard soil. Now that the people are more prosperous they are able to buy houses, so Manuel is able to use his land for building. When Luiz said Manuel is very important, he did not mean he had a lot of money. Manuel has great responsibilities and never enough cash, but he has built some wonderful houses. Some have been sold and some are for sale now. Spain has never been an easy place to live in, Claire."

She sat in silence, trying to accustom herself to this new world.

Ricardo said: "Perhaps you would like me to find you a room in the town for tonight. Perhaps you would like to go to the villa tomorrow."

She said: "I won't be such a coward as that. I will go today. But I would like you to warn her.

Just as I need time, she may need time. Would you do that? Let her decide whether she wants to see me now or not."

Ricardo paid the bill, then they walked back across the sand in silence. Claire felt her nerves tightening as they had tightened when the barman tried to send her straight to the Manzales villa. It was a fact, as Ricardo had said, that, inexplicably now, she had not thought to reply to the letter that came when she was twelve. It had borne an address, and she could have bought stamps. Would June think she deliberately handed the one that came three years later to her father? Was she going to be satisfied with her daughter's explanation of how the years between eighteen and twenty-one had slipped by without getting in touch? If, as Ricardo insinuated, June had written since and her father had confiscated the letters, would June believe that she had not known?

Unexpectedly, Ricardo took her hand. "You and I," he said, "will spend today together. I shall find you a room. Then tomorrow morning early I will telephone Juanita while Manuel is sleeping. I will tell her I am bringing a very special visitor. Manuel does not get up until midday. So you two will have a long talk together, and then you will meet Manuel when he wakes."

She was overwhelmed with gratitude at his kindness. "But don't you have to work?"

"Not today."

She wondered why, but then cast the question aside. It was unimportant in the context of what was happening. She felt the panic that had been building up in her for hours ebb away. She felt grateful to this extraordinarily handsome young brother-in-law of her mother's who appeared so wise for his years. "How can I thank you?"

"It is nothing." They had climbed up the steps below the old stone buildings on the edge of the little town. He swung her around to face him and took her hands. "I have been in love with Juanita ever since Manuel brought her home. It will be easy to look after you, for you are just a younger version of her." He lifted her hands and kissed them.

Deeply touched, embarrassed, she said lightly to cover her feelings:"My aunt thought June would be wrinkled like a prune from the sun."

Momentarily, Ricardo looked startled. Then he said gravely:"Oh yes, she is ugly. Very ugly. You will see."

They left the Hertz car in the square. Ricardo had a small sports car tucked away in a quiet street. They climbed into it and he headed out of the town on the road that ran north. At a turning a short distance along the road Ricardo turned inland. The road wound steeply in hairpin bends up the side of a brown mountain. Here and there scrubby trees grew thickly over the thin soil and then there would be a great scar of pink and gray stone, hundreds of feet high; here, an ancient landslide where green cactus grew; and there, an enclosed, high rising valley full of long grasses and ferns that grew luxuriantly because somehow they had managed to shelter from the sun.

FOUR

Up and up they went. There were chestnut trees with dark green shiny leaves, the ubiquitous cork, striped palely where the bark had been taken away and everywhere, climbing up the banks and thrusting over the edges, wild rose bushes white with blossom. Out in the green fields, hat well down over his eyes, a tired Spaniard dawdled behind two mules pulling a plough.

"Where are you taking me?" Claire asked.

"To the *finca*. 'Farm' to you."

"Your farm?"

"No. Nothing belongs to me. Our father left everything to Manuel." At her look of surprise he added: "It is the way in Spain. The eldest son looks after the rest of the family."

She said, without thinking: "But what if the eldest son wants to go off and lead a different kind of life? What happens to the family then?"

Ricardo shrugged. "That is an English question and I cannot answer it."

"You mean, the eldest son has to look after everyone whether he wants to or not?" she persisted.

"Of course he would want to look after the family," Ricardo chided her and Claire lapsed into silence, absorbing the first fragment of what she was to learn about her mother's life.

They came to the foot of a valley where the road wound alongside a chuckling stream. Gnarled olives, their leaves silver in the sun, clambered up the slopes on either side. Away in the distance, at the valley's head, a white house stood among trees. "That's it," said Ricardo.

"It seems very isolated."

"Yes."

To right and left the hills rose steeply, hemming them in. A snake who had been sunning himself in the white dust of the road scurried away as the car approached. Round another corner, lifting her head to survey the desolate hills, Claire saw a single little white painted, ocher tiled dwelling, and then, on a far ridge, another. "How do the occupants get to those houses?"

"There are roads, of sorts. You will see." And then, as they came nearer she saw that the houses were indeed tied loosely to the road by a rutted red earth ribbon of a track.

"It's wild, and surely very lonely."

"Yes. That's the importance of it," Ricardo replied. "When my troubles get on top of me I come here."

She looked up curiously. "Do you have such bad troubles?"

"Yes." His face was solemn, his eyes steadfastly on the road. "There's an old fellow who caretakes and does some work for Manuel when he can be bothered. He wants to know all about everything but he doesn't tell tales." She opened her mouth to ask what tales there were to tell, then closed it again. Ricardo grinned. "Since you don't speak Spanish he won't bother you." At the head of the valley where the road ended they came to a stop. It was a benevolent old house, two-storied, built higgledy-piggledy as though additions had been made by chance or in sudden necessity. A gable here, a sloping roof there, the windows ill-matched. Tiny dormers jutted out among the complex of roofs as though a room below had been stretched beyond endurance until the tiles were forced upwards. To fill the gaping hole, another window. The house stood on a platform of rough grass. A meandering stone staircase ran up from the road, twisting and turning among the long, neglected grasses. The terrace was built of stone. Here and there weeds grew tall through the crevasses. The huge front door that looked so impressive from the road was in fact roughly hewn from logs and studded untidily with huge iron studs.

"How incredibly quaint!" Claire exclaimed delightedly.

"A friendly house," Ricardo replied. "No one has lived here for years." He pointed to a neat cottage fifty or sixty yards away to the left. "Manuel built that for Raphael. He is seventy-two now, gnarled and beaten-up by work and the weather. He looks a hundred. His wife, too. Eulalia. She picks almonds to help out. Even from here you can see the pile of shells on the verandah." He smiled indulgently. "They never think to clear them away. Come inside." Ricardo took an enormous key from under a stone and unlocked the front door. The hinges shrieked as he pushed it wide. "I must get Raphael to oil that."

Inside was a big room, quite thirty feet long, sparsely furnished with what must be Spanish junk furniture. A table, some wooden chairs, two sofas that had probably never had pretensions to elegance and were now broken-springed as though they had suffered the high spirited capers of generations of children. The ceiling was high and heavily beamed for a floor, or floors, had been removed to form a mezzanine landing with pretty wrought iron railings, rather like a minstrels' gallery. "If I lived here," said Ricardo, "that would be my library up there. Don't you think it's given the place an air of grace?"

Oddly, it had.

"As a right-thinking architect," he went on lightly, "of course I should want to pull the whole thing down. It's a disgrace. But we love it, and it gives us something. We have our birthday parties up here sometimes. There is added excitement in the ride back round those hairpin bends with the drivers full of champagne. Some guests sleep here. There are plenty of rooms and plenty of beds. Those who have no intention of going home bring their sheets and blankets. It is always allowed."

Claire sat down on one of the lumpy sofas, her eyes on the quaint little floor above with its pretty wrought iron railing. Ricardo came and sat beside her. "You are supposed to be amused, but no, you look sad."

"I feel sad," she admitted. "And disorientated." And deprived, she might have added.

"How so?"

She needed, desperately, to talk. In a way, she needed an exorcism of all the theories and pretenses of the past. "I grew up with quite the wrong idea of what had happened to my mother," she said.

"What did you think about her?"

"That she had run off with a penniless rascal who had to support an enormous family."

Ricardo chuckled. "That's right. Manuel was a rascal to run off with a married woman. So, you have the picture right. What is worrying you, Claire?"

She flushed and looked away. Then, when she realized Ricardo was still waiting she added: "We're talking on different levels."

He said shrewdly: "You thought she would be scrubbing the clothes on stones in the river? Living in a hovel? Juanita has never had to do anything like that. Even when Manuel was very poor she had two servants."

"You have to be rich to have two servants in England."

"I know. There are not the peasants."

She felt embarrassed. "Tell me about your family," she said.

He watched her thoughtfully for a moment, his brown hands on his knees. Then he said: "No, because I am biased. You must make up your own mind about them. Or perhaps hear about them from your mother. I am going to see old Eulalia and ask her if she will cook a meal for us this evening. What would you like to do now? Walk in the hills?"

"I'd love that. But Ricardo, you must tell me about your family. I want to be prepared for them. And for my mother."

"No," he repeated quite firmly; disappointed, she knew it would be no use protesting.

They walked up to the ridge behind the house. There were higher and higher mountains behind. Ricardo told her about Spain. He told her little things about the family, too, but not very much. She picked an armful of wild flowers—long-stemmed irises, delicate cyclamens, honey-scented roses, and set them in a stone urn she found in one of the downstairs rooms. Raphael, a toothless cinder of a man, brought them wine and his wife Eulalia came with goat stew and crusty bread, green salad made startlingly beautiful with sliced red peppers, and a bowl of figs and wild cherries. "I've never tasted goat before."

"You like it?"

"Yes, I think so. It's strong, but nice."

They ate on the stone terrace looking down the length of the valley, watching the shadows form as the sun went down. And then it was dark and Raphael shambled out with a lantern. Insects swirled round it and moths, maddened by the light, spun crazily, smashing their frail bodies at the glass. It was romantic and peaceful and a little unreal. Claire felt immensely close to Ricardo and she knew her feelings were not merely gratitude. There had been an affinity between them from the beginning, something she had never felt before with another man. Later, they went inside, taking the lantern with them, and Ricardo took her on a tour of the upstairs rooms. "We should have done it by daylight," he said, "but you will be able to see what there is to see. There's not very much." He spoke the truth. Old iron bedsteads, old and rickety tables, occasional chairs with the leather worn away. On the way back they paused at the top of the staircase. Ricardo put the lantern down on the floor. He leaned back against the banisters saying quizzically: "Well? Do you feel more acclimatized? Are you ready to face whatever lies in store for you?"

Impulsively, Claire reached out to him and he took her hands. Something hot and passionate from the night sprang between them. "You've helped so much. How can I ever thank you?"

As though supplying the answer, Ricardo slipped his arms round her. She lifted her face in what seemed the most natural gesture. Then suddenly the magic was smashed by a stern voice coming up from below: "Ricardo, I have been waiting for you. Come down, please, and bring your friend with you."

They sprang apart as though a saber had come between them. Claire gasped. Ricardo swore softly under his breath. "It's Manuel."

Claire swung round and looked down the stairs into the big room below. He was seated on one of the broken-down sofas and he was presently in the act of lighting a cigarette. It was not quite dark. In the dim light filtering through the open door Claire could see the shape of him: a giant of a man with luxuriant black hair. Ricardo picked up the lantern, indicated that Claire descend the stairs, then when she hesitated, half-paralyzed with fright, he led the way.

Manuel's eyes were on him as though deliberately excluding the girl, exonerating her from blame. She could tell by the way he sat smoking, casual in a disciplined manner, that he was controlling his anger while at the same time drawing attention to it. He said heavily: "I didn't get your message, Ricardo. That's why I was surprised to find you here."

"I didn't send a message." Ricardo, though clearly taken aback, had regained his poise. He spoke in a clipped, cool voice. "I came unexpectedly."

"Are you not going to introduce me to your friend before you go?" The inference was stark and insulting. Claire could see him clearly now. His great head with its rich mane of hair gave him a patriarchal air, but with dark eyes narrowed, brows lowered, he looked a man who would strike fear into the most dauntless person. Ricardo made no reply. He placed the lamp on the table. Manuel spoke directly to Claire in brief, clipped Spanish. She replied: "I am English. I don't understand."

Unmoved by the fact that she had actually understood the words addressed to Ricardo, Manuel said: "Then you have heard my wishes. I am sorry to have to send you away, but it is not possible for you to stay here tonight. My brother had no right to bring you. This is not his property."

Ricardo was making signs to her to keep quiet but she replied angrily: "There was never any question of my staying here tonight. Ricardo merely brought me up to see the house." She saw the agony in Ricardo's eyes, the lifted head, and knew he would prefer her to leave silently, without excuses.

Suddenly Ricardo leaned forward and, picking up the lantern, held it close to Claire's face. There was a zinging silence. Flustered by Ricardo's act, Claire swung round to him, then compulsively back. Manuel dropped his cigarette on the floor and forgot to stamp it out. Thumping one large hand on the low table, he sprang to his feet. For all his size, he was a very athletic man. "You're Claire! You're Claire!" Manuel exclaimed delightedly. "You're Juanita's daughter!" In that startled moment Claire's anger evaporated. In two short strides Manuel stood in front of her and placing one hand on either side of her face, kissed her. "The little Claire." Then he rounded angrily on his brother. "How dare you bring her up here! How dare you!"

Ricardo's face had gone hard again. He stood tall, as tall as his brother but with half his bulk, his handsome head arrogantly high. Claire had a very certain feeling that Ricardo held his hands in check and his tongue. That if this man were not the head of his family she would have been witnessing a brawl.

Manuel said sternly: "You will take Claire to her mother immediately, Ricardo. She has been waiting a long time."

"No! She does not know I'm here!"

Manuel's face softened. "Nineteen years she has waited."

"Yes, I see. Of course."

Ricardo's blue eyes flashed, but he said in a controlled voice: "Claire wanted to go in the morning, Manuel."

"She will go now," said Manuel with complete authority. "You will stop at *La Fragata* to telephone so that Juanita will be prepared."

Claire felt unstrung. She could not understand why Ricardo did not explain their circumstances and why he clearly did not want her to explain. Perhaps only because he knew Manuel would not believe them. In the event they went rather like two sheepish and obedient children, down the long, stepped incline. The moon had not yet risen and they could see little beyond the pale glow of the stones. Ricardo opened the passenger door and she slipped into the car. She could feel the strength of his anger then, as he joined her. It was in the lusty crash of the door behind him, in the clang of his keys as he blundered with the ignition, in the fierce hunching of his spare shoulders. She wanted to ask him if he always obeyed his brother like that, but she did not dare.

They drove in silence down the dark valley, then up over a hill and down into another valley where the lights of a village showed. Ricardo pulled up outside a bar with the name *La Fragata* stamped across the front of the striped awning. A dozen or so men were seated at small tables on the pavement. A feeling of panic came over Claire then and she exploded: "Do you have to obey him to the letter? It will disturb my mother if I turn up at this hour. I want to go in the morning."

"I am sorry," said Ricardo, then added simply: "This is Spain."

"Meaning, I have been compromised and must be known to have a chaperon for the rest of the night?" she flared. "You've got to be joking."

"Juanita would be upset if she knew you were

with me," Ricardo said resignedly and climbed out of the car.

"What are you going to say to her?"

"Only that you are here and I am bringing you along."

Claire sat in the car waiting pensively and a little nervously while he telephoned. There was clearly something more to the dissolution of the evening's idyll and to Ricardo's strange obedience that sat so uncomfortably on his shoulders, than met the eye. She was angry, too, at being forced into disturbing her mother at this hour. She glanced at her watch. It was after ten. She supposed she would now have to make up a tale about arriving late. She did not want to start the relationship with lies. She saw Ricardo emerge through the open doorway with the colored plastic ribbons that formed a curtain dancing in his wake. The tense anger had gone to be replaced by a faintly puzzled expression.

"What did she say?" Claire asked anxiously.

He dropped lightly into his seat. "There was no reply. But we'll go anyway. She must be somewhere round. Perhaps with a neighbor."

"Perhaps she's gone out to dinner."

"She would not do that without Manuel."

They transferred Claire's luggage to Ricardo's car and in cool defiance of her protests Ricardo pocketed her keys. "I will arrange for the car to be collected," he said.

"But I will need it. I must be independent," Claire protested.

"No," he replied. "You are with your family now. You will not need independence. Of course you will be taken wherever you want to go."

Her chagrin melted into the general disturbance within her. They drove out of the little
town and round the bay, then up a steep, winding
hill. "I wish I was arriving in daylight. I don't even
know where I am." She was becoming unnerved.

"You will know soon enough. The house is one
of a complex Manuel and Leopoldo have build."

"Leopoldo?"

"My brother. He is a builder."

"Oh."

They rounded a hairpin bend. In the car lights a
high stone wall appeared on the hillside.
Luxuriant creepers trailed down almost to the
road. Ricardo swung the wheel hard left and ran
into a wide drive. There was a pair of enormous
garages with the kind of doors that swing up and
out of sight. The space inside would take four
cars. Side by side stood a small Fiat and a Range-
Rover.

Claire climbed out. The moon had risen and she
could see quite clearly now. They were in a sort of
courtyard with the garages on one side and on the
other a high wall from which hung great av-
alanches of green vine. There was pink bougainvillaea and a slash of dark red that looked in the
half-light like geraniums, a weeping willow and
two enormous palms. The sweet smell of hon-
eysuckle was everywhere.

"Come," said Ricardo. He led her into another
courtyard, also enclosed and equally heavily
overhung with vines and flowers. There was a
glass door ahead and set at either side, an urn
overflowing with trailing pink geraniums, their
petals waxy in the moonlight.

Claire asked in surprise: "Where are we? Is this

a house? You said they lived in a complex." She had expected stark brick villas side by side.

"This is Manuel's house, and it is in a complex," Ricardo replied, amused at her astonishment. "But he had a very clever architect. The houses are built around a little knoll placed so that not one can see another."

She looked up at him sharply, sensing from the deprecating laugh in his voice that he had been the architect.

Ricardo opened the glass door and called: "Juanita." There was no reply. He switched on a light. They were in a square hall. Wide wooden stairs ran to the upper floor. There were bookshelves everywhere and photographs, and pictures on walls. "Juanita!" Ricardo called again.

"There's no one here," said Claire. "The house is empty. I can feel it." Ricardo ran a hand through his dark hair. He looked disturbed. "Why shouldn't she be having supper with a neighbor?"

"Manuel would have known."

"Perhaps the invitation came after he left. Why don't you call up some of her friends?"

"I'll go next door," acceded Ricardo. "Wait here."

Claire stood in the middle of the hall, looking around. Beyond lay a big drawing room. She crossed to the door and flicked the switch. A small chandelier flooded the room with light. It was a beautiful, comfortable room with an enormous stone fireplace, and everywhere there were more bookshelves, photographs and pictures. The big sofa was burdened with a shower of colorful cushions and the chairs were low and deep. On the floor was a bright Moorish carpet in geometrical flower design. She went to look at the photo-graphs. One of Manuel, handsome in evening dress. A boy with fair hair and olive skin. That must be one of her half-brothers. Then Claire gasped. It was like looking at herself! This must be June, the girl with a baby in her arms and a small child beside her. She had the same fair hair, the same broad forehead, the same straight nose. Only the mouth was different. Where Claire's mouth was wide and generous, her mother's was soft, vulnerable and passionate. Even the broken hairline where the hair curled in short tendrils was the same. She stared at the likeness, amused, as-tonished. No wonder Manuel had recognized her at a glance! There were pictures of June and her children everywhere in silver, leather and velvet frames. A spacious kitchen went off this room at right angles.

The dining room led off both the kitchen and the drawing room for there were no passageways, and both of them opened on to a wide verandah with a tiled overhang. Before her now, across the small lawn, the pale tiles of a swimming pool gleamed in the moonlight and beyond that two statues and a small marble lion. The house, Claire could see now, was built in the shape of a V, enclosing the lawn and pool.

Her mother had, indeed, all the comforts. Claire was glad, but she was angry, too. And upset. She was still standing there, emotionally disturbed, when Ricardo returned. His face was creased into worry lines. "She cannot have gone far," he said. "Her car is there."

Then Claire saw the note. It was propper up

against a bowl of fruit on a low table on the verandah and she could just see it, a pale square in the semidarkness. She went through the open door and picked it up. There was no envelope. The words were in Spanish. She handed it to Ricardo.

FIVE

He read the note in silence. Momentarily, his face was stricken, then a forced smile appeared. He said lightly: "She has gone away for a few days, that is all."

"Without telling her husband?" Claire waited for a reply but Ricardo seemd incapable of making one. "You mean she has run away?" Claire continued sharply, then the shock disintegrated in an hysterical little laugh. "It can't be. I mean, the odds must be a thousand million to one that a mother should happen to run off the very day her discarded daughter turns up."

"You told her you were coming? You wrote?" Ricardo seemed stunned.

"No."

"Then she does not know. Besides," Ricardo said gently, "she has longed to have you all these years. Why would she run when you are coming?"

"Who knows what people will do in a crisis? Panic, perhaps. That man Luiz at the bar who telephoned you must have called her, also."

"No, he would not do that."

"Why not? Some people like to be first with news. Now that I've seen pictures of my mother I realize Luiz recognized me. Is it generally known in the town that June Manzales has an English daughter?"

"Y-yes."

"Then surely this is what's happened. My mother could have panicked. Perhaps she has a guilty conscience about me. About not coming to England to see me when she could so easily afford to do so. It does seem odd," said Claire with a touch of bitterness.

"She could not go to England." Ricardo rushed to the defense of his sister-in-law. "Your father had custody and he insisted that there should be no tug-of-war over you. He thought it would be very bad for a child to be switched back and forth between parents," Ricardo spoke oddly, with feeling.

"He knew jolly well I wouldn't want to go back to live with him after I had visited my mother," retorted Claire angrily, turning to the photograph of June Manzales with her baby in her arms, the face so soft and sweet. "Even if he didn't have a true picture of her circumstances, he did know her." The anger was for her father but Ricardo reacted as though it had been directed at him.

"She had no choice. The English judge was cruel. Inhuman. She had no choice," he repeated.

"Let's not argue about something that happened when I was two and you weren't much older," said Claire, suddenly feeling weary and sad. "Perhaps my coming has nothing to do with her departure." Ricardo was staring down at the paper in his hand, looking disturbed. "What does it say? It's really not fair of you to take advantage of the fact that I don't speak the language."

Momentarily, it looked as though Ricardo would translate the wording. Then: "It is for Manuel," he said.

"You've read it," she pointed out, injured. Again, there was no reply. After a moment Claire said: "Tell me, Ricardo, why was the door open? The front door of the house, I mean?"

"It is always open. No one comes, except the maids. And friends, of course."

"Oh. So, what are you going to do?"

"There is no telephone at the *finca*," Ricardo said. "I must go and tell Manuel."

Claire picked up her handbag. "I'll come with you."

"No. You must stay here."

"Stay here?" Claire echoed incredulously. "Catch me staying in a strange open house in a strange country all by myself at night!" Suddenly a new and rather sinister thought struck her. "How do you know June hasn't been forced to write that note? How do you know, come to think of it, she hasn't been abducted?" Ricardo looked down at Claire, faintly amused. At the same time there was deep concern behind his eyes. "Because of what it says, I guess." Claire answered her own question pointedly, and waited. Ricardo's face was troubled and for a moment she thought he was going to tell her what was in the note but suddenly he thrust it into a pocket in his shirt. "If you don't want to take me to the farm, or *finca*, or whatever it is," she began again when it became evident there would be no reply, "then please drop me off in the town and I'll find somewhere to stay." She looked at her watch and exclaimed in dismay: "It's midnight! What point is there in waking Manuel at this time?"

"I think he is going to Granada on business in the morning. It is better I stop him. He must come back here."

"And who will take me in at this hour? Only a five star hotel will accept a guest at midnight. I'm sure there's no first-class accommodation in such a little place."

Ricardo said: "You may have my room. I will return to sleep here."

"That seems a lot of unnecessary bother. Why can't we both sleep here?"

Ricardo's eyes flickered and his well-cut mouth twitched. "It would not be correct."

"Heavens!"

"Yes, Spain is old-fashioned," Ricardo admitted, "and this is a very small town where everyone knows everyone else's business."

"Of course. I understand." An association of ideas triggered off something in her mind. What business had Manuel at the farm tonight? In the dark, one does not check on crops, or animals. And it was not as though he was getting ready for an early start to work tomorrow because Ricardo had said he was going to Granada. "It occurs to me," she said carefully, "that Manuel's car wasn't parked beside yours when we left the *finca*. Where was it?"

Ricardo shrugged.

"Could it be that there was a woman in it, and therefore it was parked somewhere out of sight?"

Ricardo looked momentarily startled. Then he said: "Oh come, Claire."

"Is that why you won't read the note out to me?" she persisted. "Because my mother knew Manuel was having an *affaire*? Is this why she's run away? You may as well tell me, Ricardo. If I'm to stay I shall find out. And I'd like to get the picture now."

Ricardo looked uncomfortable. "No. No, you're wrong." But his blue eyes were hooded. "Manuel is a good husband," he said.

"I'm sure he is a good provider. It doesn't follow that a good provider's faithful. You're very loyal, Ricardo, but I can see there's something bugging you. I wish you'd tell me what it is. *Is* Manuel faithful?"

"He is faithful to Juanita in his heart," Ricardo replied gravely.

Claire began a laugh, but the sincerity in this Spaniard's eyes arrested it. "I'm not certain that's enough for an English woman," she said unhappily. "Please take me back to the *finca* with you. I've no intention of going into the house and getting proof of Manuel's peccadilloes, they're not my affair. I'll wait in the car. Then let's come back here to sleep. Who will know? We're cut off behind walls and trees. And it's so late that we wouldn't be seen."

He was looking at her oddly, a flicker in those very attractive eyes.

"It's not an invitation to share my bed, I assure you," Claire asserted hurriedly, half-laughing, half-annoyed. "But I honestly cannot see why we shouldn't share the same house."

"Manuel wouldn't like it."

"The hell with Manuel," Claire exploded. "I don't like what I suspect he might be up to and you're not putting my mind at rest. Clearly my mother didn't like it, either, or she wouldn't have skipped off. Now that you've found me not quite so dumb as you expected, perhaps you'll read me the note."

Ricardo turned away, patently disturbed. He seemed about to say something, then stopped. The note stayed safely in his pocket. "I told you Manuel is faithful to Juanita in his heart. He doesn't conduct *affaires*, but it is true, he likes pretty women, and you cannot cure a man of that."

"That's Spanish philosophy, is it?"

"I don't know. We Spanish think differently from the English. Juanita has not learned, truly learned, even in nineteen years, how important is the family. I don't believe God cares about what you call peccadilloes," declared Ricardo with a flash of arrogance. "Surely if you love, that is what is important. Manuel loves Juanita. He loves us all. When you know my brother you will feel differently about him."

There seemed no answer. Feeling chastened, and surprised that she should be so, Claire swung her shoulder bag over her arm. "Come on. Let's go and tell Manuel the bad news."

It was all darkness and flashing car lights. They did not talk much on the winding road back to the farm. Ricardo left Claire in the car and went off up the long line of steps. The house might have been empty. There was no chimney smoke, no light. She saw Ricardo's flashlight flicker in the doorway and then there was darkness again. A few moments later he returned, the flashlight jabbing and darting like a small, bright animal. "I left the note," he said as he climbed in beside her. "I put it on the table where he cannot miss it in the morning."

Of course. What else could he do? Ricardo turned the car around. There was still no sign of Manuel's vehicle. Now that the first shock was over Claire felt sick with disappointment and her fury against Manuel was a living thing. "Perhaps my mother needs me more than I need her now," she said as they ran off down the hill.

"Juanita needs you," agreed Ricardo.

Surprised by his gentle words, she swung round to look at him. "Are you by any chance in love with my mother?" she asked, abrasive because she was shaken.

"I love her," he replied simply, and then, making Claire feel ashamed: "she is my sister."

It was nearly two o'clock when they arrived back on the outskirts of the sleeping town. The car slowed. Claire said sharply, nervously: "I'm not going to stay in your room and start more complications. There's your landlady to consider, and the town gossips. Besides, my suitcase is at the villa." Ricardo did not reply but the car was still losing pace. He took a left hand turn that brought them in to the road they had taken when they left the square. Claire said: "I mean that. I will not stay in your room."

"No, no. Of course. But I must collect something. Some pajamas." She did not believe him, but there was no point in saying so.

On the outskirts of the square the car pulled up. Over to the left there was a little bar, still open, the lights glowing. "Let's have a drink first, shall we? We're both upset." And it was true, Ricardo now looked infinitely disturbed. Perhaps he wanted to talk to her. Perhaps he would, after all, tell her what was in the note.

"I've heard Spaniards like to stay up all night." She smiled a little. "Your friend Luiz said Manuel doesn't go to bed until well into the morning."

"I don't keep Manuel's hours. Just tonight, I am not ready to sleep. There is much to consider."

There certainly was. Perhaps a drink would do her good, too.

Ricardo put an arm around Claire as they crossed the pavement. She smiled up at him. "It's not so bad. Nothing is ever as bad as it looks," he said soothingly and squeezed her arm. Oddly, in some queer, extra-dimensional way, she felt as though she had known this strange Spaniard half a lifetime, yet without understanding him.

There were perhaps a dozen men in the bar, and a blonde girl. Ricardo led her to a table in a corner. The patrons, who all appeared to know Ricardo, nodded, eyeing Claire curiously. The barman was conducting a passionate argument with a shortish, thickset man who had his back to them. Claire sat down. "What will you have?" Ricardo asked.

"A glass of wine, please."

Someone attracted the barman's attention. He

concluded the argument with a flourish and came down the length of the bar to shake hands. "What do you want, Ricardo?" He nodded courteously, smilingly, across the room to Claire.

The man with whom the barman had been conducting the argument turned slowly around. He was very dark, with a low forehead and heavy brows that hung so far over his eyes the eyes themselves seemed half-closed. As though he had got the worst of the argument, his face was tight and angry. He surveyed Claire deliberately, rudely, the anger seemingly transferring itself to her, and then from her to Ricardo. Ricardo, following her look, nodded briefly, then turned away. The man picked up his glass and came to stand beside the table, looking down at Claire. He spoke sharply in Spanish across the room to Ricardo. Ricardo flashed an angry reply, gesturing to him to leave Claire alone. Instead, the man drew out a chair. Ricardo, his face tight, spoke to the barman, came back to the table and helped Claire to her feet. "Come, we will not stay here." He led her swiftly outside. She could feel anger in the rigid muscles in his arm, the tight closing of his fingers over hers.

"What was that all about?" she asked as they reached the car.

"The man is a nuisance. I'm sorry." Ricardo brushed a hand angrily through his dark hair. "It was bad luck to choose that bar. Come, let's go back to the villa, after all."

"He looked at you in a threatening manner. As though he hated you," she said and shivered involuntarily.

"Fernando Pascual hates everybody," retorted

Ricardo brusquely. "That's the way of him. You saw he was arguing with the barman when we arrived. Come." He held the car door open.

Claire sat immersed in thought, watching Ricardo's profile as he drove. She did not entirely accept the fact that the man Fernando had picked on them simply because they were new arrivals in the bar. The expression in his eyes when he looked at Ricardo had been more a look of warning than of hate. She wondered whether her own presence had anything to do with the ill-feeling engendered. They sped along the beach front, then up the dark and silent hill. Ricardo turned in at the driveway, parked the car beside the Fiat, then closed the garage doors carefully as they had not been closed before.

"Okay," he said. "I will stay," but he looked unhappy.

Claire tried to laugh about it. "Are you afraid of your reputation, or mine?"

He did not answer, merely shrugging as he led the way into the house. At the foot of the stairs he turned and took her hands. "This has been a bad start for you, Claire. A very bad start altogether. Let's sit for a while and talk. I can see you're upset. You probably wouldn't sleep if you did go to bed."

"Okay." She met his eyes sympathetically. It was Ricardo, she felt certain, who would be unable to sleep. She wished she knew why.

"I'll get a drink," he said. "What would you like?"

"What is there?"

Ricardo smiled. "A big choice. I will have coffee and a brandy."

Brandy! She did not think she could. "What about cocoa?" she asked.

He shook his head. "I'm sorry. Juanita's eating habits are no longer English. But there is milk. Perhaps a little whisky in it?"

She made a face. "Straight milk, please. But let's warm it, shall we?"

They went into the kitchen together. It was a big room with lots of windows. There was a rocking chair and a scrubbed table with a top as thick as a butcher's slab. In a corner was a small, elegant table around which were grouped half a dozen leather-topped stools. An enormous deep freeze took up part of one wall and there was a great square-fronted refrigerator. Claire gave a little gasp of surprise and delight. Across the two doors of the refrigerator a street scene had been painted, Parisian in flavor, with old balconied houses, tall windows, and black wrought iron work. On the pavements quaint figures strolled, some in berets, some with old-fashioned sunshades. "How absolutely wonderful," she exclaimed. "Who did that?"

"It's my work, of course." He spoke with a mixture of pride and amusement.

"But how clever! And how nice of them to allow you to do it."

Ricardo took a bottle of milk from the refrigerator. "For the Spaniard the kitchen is the center of the house."

"I thought you ate out most of the time."

"That's true. But when we're at home we like to have the family around us, watching the cook and giving advice and drinking wine. Even the children, perhaps, doing their homework. Now, here is some coffee already made. I will have to heat it."

"Great. Where are the boys, Ricardo?"

"They're weekly boarders at a school in Malaga."

"So you have four days in which to find June."

He nodded. "Yes. She will come back, for she loves Manuel. It's her way of trying to make him understand how she feels."

Standing uneasily in the middle of the kitchen with its beautifully polished wood cupboards, Claire surveyed its modern comfort. "Manuel is certainly not a penniless Spaniard now. This is a most beautiful villa."

"It was designed by me, built by Leopoldo, and planned and paid for by Manuel. Juanita was not allowed to see it until it was built."

"Not allowed to see her own house?" Claire asked incredulously.

"Ah! You see how Spanish Juanita has become, really," Ricardo said. "Here in Spain Manuel's type does everything and the woman acquiesces." Ricardo watched Claire with a little smile, as though waiting for her to protest about women's rights. "They lived on the hill opposite when Juanita first came here, in a tiny apartment. Then Manuel told her he would build her a beautiful house over on this hillside where the almond blossom would be seen in the spring from every window, but that she must not go up to see it until it was finished."

"It sounds very poetic and romantic," Claire conceded, "but surely she wanted to plan her own house?"

"She was satisfied. She knows her man. Come,

the milk is hot now. We will go out onto the verandah and talk there. I must be the one to tell about the family now." Ricardo handed her an enormous cup and she followed him through the narrow dining room and out onto the verandah. There were no passages in this part of the house. While Ricardo went to get his brandy Claire sat down on a cane chair and put her milk and cookies on a small, glass-topped table. Across the lawn the swimming-pool lay like a blue picture in its pale tiled frame. In front of them a thick-trunked, squat palm tree spread its drooping fronds. Ricardo joined her. "That tree," he said, "came to Juanita in a pot four years ago. Now the upper fronds touch the bedroom windows. You will be surprised to see how plants grow in Spain."

Faintly, in the pale moonlight, she could see the abundant creepers that fell heavily across every wall and the air was full of the scent of flowers. "The penniless Spanish bandit," Claire murmured to herself, laughing a little, ruefully. "This was the great thing. That my mother had thrown herself away on a peasant."

"Peasant?" She saw the swiftly uplifted head, the sudden already familiar flash of arrogance in the eyes and added quickly: "I mean, a very poor man."

"What man of twenty has made his way?" Ricardo asked. "My father was not wealthy. He had planted many almond trees. They are over there on the hillside opposite," Ricardo gestured towards the outer stone wall. "They are beautiful, Juanita's great joy and delight. But they do not bring in a lot of money. Everyone was poor when

Juanita came and there was no point in building houses because no one could afford to buy them. Manuel planted olives, but they say you plant olives for your grandchildren, not for yourself, for it is a long time before they bear. He has also planted a lot of avocado pear trees up at the *finca*. Those trees will be a great source of income now that more restaurants and fancy hotels are springing up along the coast. The locals, too, are learning to eat avocado pears. But it is the houses that must make Manuel's fortune. Foreigners are coming to live farther up the coast to get away from the crush at Marbella and Malaga, and also, as Spain prospers, more Spaniards are able to afford houses on the coast."

"Yes, I see. And you—you work for him?"

"No." There was an odd, flat tone to the denial.

"With him?"

"No."

"But you designed this house."

"In the beginning, I worked with him. But I must lead my own life. I cannot allow myself to be eaten up by Manuel," Ricardo said, surprising her.

"Tonight, when Manuel ordered us out of his farmhouse, why did you not explain what we were doing there? Is he the sort of person one cannot talk to?"

"No. Not all. You will love Manuel for his own sake when you get to know him. Everyone comes to him for help and advice. Not just the family. Elderly English ladies who live in the bay come to him, and even people in out-flung villages, locals and foreigners. At only thirty-nine, Manuel is a grand patriarchal figure. A rock the size of Gibraltar."

"Oh?" she asked dryly.

"A rock," he said. "He will still be here when Juanita returns. That is what counts, is it not?"

Claire thought for a moment, then said emotionally: "I see your rock from another angle. Totally unyielding." Perhaps a woman who was unlucky with one husband was bound to be unlucky with the next. A bad chooser. Ricardo did not answer and a little later she said: "Tell me, how do you propose to find my mother?"

"She will not abandon her children," he replied with quiet confidence. "She will be at the school to pick them up on Friday afternoon."

"And bring them home? That sounds too complacent by half."

He shrugged, smiling again. "Maybe she will want to take them with her. But at least Manuel will catch her collecting them. Or, if she sends for the boys they will be able to give him the address."

She eyed Ricardo thoughtfully. "You're very confident."

"First and foremost, Juanita is a mother," said Ricardo with total conviction. "She would not let a child down."

Claire felt her face tighten. She glanced away. A moment passed then Ricardo's hand was on hers and he was saying: "I'm sorry, Claire."

She shrugged, but the emotion was still there, deep down, crucifying her. "It's been quite a day," she said lightly. She stood up. She had wondered for a while if he had something to tell her. Now, he may have had second thoughts, or misgivings as to the wisdom of it. She rose, yawning. It was too late. She felt physically and emotionally drained. "Do you know what room would be likely to be allotted to me?"

He nodded. "I'll carry your bag up." They ascended the stairs together. At the top he turned right. "This guestroom." He opened a door and switched on the light. "There will be sheets on the bed. Juanita keeps it made up in case guests come unexpectedly." She thought it astonishing that Ricardo could make so free with his brother's house, but she was too tired to care. She scarcely saw the room. A bed, a dressing table, and through the door, a pink bathroom. "Thanks, Ricardo. You've been very kind."

"Sleep well." He went back towards the stairs. Tired as she was, she was suddenly aware of his direction and ran after him. "Ricardo! You're not going!"

He turned to look at her whimsically. "I am going to borrow some pajamas from Manuel's room. I did not get them from my room, remember."

"Oh." She stopped, feeling foolish and with something more in her mind. "You really have been most kind." He stepped forward and took her face in his hands. "Can I have that kiss now?" he asked softly.

She hesitated, edgy and confused. "Because I am so like June? Or because you're sorry for me?"

"Neither," he replied. "Perhaps to show my gratitude. You have arrived in answer to a prayer."

She was thinking that at an earlier hour this was just where Manuel came in. Ricardo kissed her, gently at first, and then harder. She broke away, frightened. Not, curiously, frightened of him but of herself, for the inexplicable emotion that had filled her when she first saw him in the square was creeping over her again. As though her destiny lay here, and there was to be no escaping.

S I X

Claire wakened to a blaze of sunlight. At four o'clock in the morning it had not seemed necessary to draw the curtains. She rose and went over to the window. The garden was empty, the pool a glittering aquamarine square in the emerald green lawn. Over the creeper-hung walls and away out to sea two small fishing boats scudded landwards. Claire listened, but there was no sound in the house. She rummaged in her bag for a bikini and slipped it on, brushed her hair and went downstairs. From the kitchen came the clink of china. She crossed the hall calling, "Ricardo."

A heavy-featured woman with short legs and a lot of dark hair tied at the nape of her neck looked around the kitchen door in surprise. She addressed Claire volubly in Spanish. Claire stopped her with a gesture. "I don't understand." She went back upstairs and looked in at all the bedroom doors. They were empty, and not one showed signs of having been slept in. She shivered, wondering whether Ricardo had, after all, left her on her own, or if he had merely tidied up meticulously in the morning before leaving.

She dived into the pool and swam two lengths. The servant was coming across the coarse grass carrying a small tray. She stood beside the pool with a puzzled expression on her brown face. As Claire climbed out she showered questions on her. Claire squeezed the water from her hair, took the tray and smiling, said: "Thank you so much. I'm sorry. I don't speak Spanish." The woman went back to the kitchen, looking depressed. There was a plastic packet of dry French toast on the tray and two little plates with butter and jam.

Claire went to a small, white-painted table and placing her chair where she could see the almond blossom as well as the sea, poured the coffee then drank it slowly, wondering what on earth she was going to do. With no transport and her inability to speak the language, what could she do but wait until someone turned up?

Why had she allowed Ricardo to confiscate the keys of her Hertz car? The low stone wall cut off the sharp spring breeze that brought in the scent of almond blossom from the hillside where the pink flowers billowed and frothed with unearthly beauty. Behind and above, far up the high hill, a little group of houses were clustered in the Spanish way. Looking after each other, Claire thought uncomfortably, as Manuel is said to look after his family. Over in the east and far below a lone yacht, its white sails filled, headed up the coast towards Almeria.

She crossed the coarse, spiky Spanish grass to the wing of the house which she had not visited the night before. The glass doors stood open and she could see through to a long room with a big desk covered in papers, more bookshelves, a child's rocking horse, more pictures on the walls. Manuel's study, perhaps?

She went back to the pool and sat down with her feet in the water. Inside the villa the telephone was ringing. The servant called to her. "Señorita!"

That must be Ricardo. With a little gasp of relief and pleasure she ran. "Ricardo."

"Hello. You're up."

"What's more, I've had breakfast and a swim. Did you stay last night?"

"Of course."

"Thank you. Ricardo, please explain to the servant here who I am. She—"

"I've done that. Don't worry."

"Thanks. Where's Manuel?"

"I haven't heard from him. I'll come up. I'll be there in ten minutes."

She replaced the receiver thoughtfully. Before she could move away it rang again. Automatically, she lifted it. "Hello." The voice belonged to a woman. She was speaking in Spanish. June? Overcome with emotion, Claire managed to say: "Can you speak English, please?"

"Who is that?" The voice was faintly accented. Claire knew immediately it belonged to a Spaniard and her heart plummeted.

"I am a—a guest. Who do you want?"

"It is for Ricardo that I ring," the woman told

her. "This is Rosita. If he comes to the villa, be pleased to tell him to come to me."

"Oh yes. Y-yes."

"Thank you."

Claire replaced the receiver, then because her legs were shaking, she sat down on the seat beside the telephone. Is this how I am going to react when I actually speak to June? Rosita! Was Ricardo married, then? Nothing, she told herself unsteadily, would surprise her now. She went back to the pool and sat staring into the water, feeling depressed. Twenty minutes later Ricardo came jauntily across the grass, smiling, his black hair gleaming in the sunlight. He bent over her, lifted one of her hands and kissed it. "That's wonderful," she laughed. "I love having my hand kissed." Suddenly excited, she scrambled to her feet. "Have you brought your trunks?"

His eyes were approvingly on her slim figure. "Yes."

The servant emerged from the verandah carrying a long terrycloth robe over one arm. Wearing a polite but disapproving expression on her face, she handed it to Claire. Repressing an astonished smile, Claire thanked her gravely and slipped the robe around her shoulders. "You'll have to read me the book of rules. I don't want to offend." Suddenly there was an edge to her voice. "It's okay to go off for a bit of hanky-panky in the hills with someone else's husband, but you don't sit with your—what are you, Ricardo? Step-uncle?—in your bikini."

He smiled, not at all offended. "Manuel is old-fashioned."

"Yes, isn't he? I'm a bit out of my depth here. I

hope you'll forgive my curiosity, but the question is pertinent. Are you married?"

Ricardo chuckled. "Why would you ask that?" And then, without waiting for a reply: "I'll go and get my trunks."

"Perhaps only because you kissed me twice in an empty house." She realized now how disturbed she had been by the tone of authority in the voice of the woman named Rosita.

Ricardo turned, pretending to be hurt, laughing a little, and with something else in his manner that puzzled her. "Now, that is unkind. I'm not married."

"Yes. I'm sorry. It was unkind."

He went inside, leaving her wondering why she had not told him about the telephone call. Feeling guilty. When he returned she was back in the water again. "What are you going to do about getting June back?" she asked.

He dived in and swam fast to the end of the pool and back. He was a strong swimmer.

"I don't see that there is anything anyone can do except wait until she contacts the children. Her car is here. That means she's determined not to be traced. She won't have gone far," Ricardo told Claire confidently. "Perhaps, anyway, she will return before the weekend."

"And what shall I do now?"

"Wait for Manuel."

"D'you think he may bother to return?" she found herself asking abrasively.

Ricardo placed both hands on her shoulders. "Please, Claire, don't be angry. Manuel would know there is nothing he can do. I expect he has gone to Granada if his business was important, but be sure he will return to talk to you as soon as possible."

Claire said with conviction: "I'm too angry to talk to him. I think I, too, will go away until my mother returns."

"Please don't go. Manuel would be very upset if you were to leave."

"I can't see myself haunting the villa in this very respectable robe for the next four days." She looked down at the garment, suddenly realizing it must belong to June. The thought disturbed her. It seemed all wrong to be wearing June's clothes when June had disappeared. And she could not understand this strange, emotional seesaw that she seemed to be riding with Ricardo, moving close, then swinging away, compulsively attracted, yet with something between them forming a block, and this frightening feeling of destiny. "My rented car is still in the town," she said. "Obviously I can't go and see the boys for they'll ask about their mother, but I feel inclined to go off to a hotel." She didn't look at him as she said: "I can let you know the address and June can send for me when she returns."

Ricardo said persuasively: "You must meet the family, Claire."

"No. I don't want to." She had a strange feeling of being trapped. There was the disapproving servant. The man who had driven them out of the bar. Manuel's strength. She was afraid to be here when he returned. "I think I'll go and pack." She started across the lawn at a run, then swung back. "By the way," she added, and was shaken to find her voice charged with emotion, "someone called

Rosita rang up. She wants to see you. It sounded important."

Ricardo did not reply. It was as though he had not heard. She waited.

"Okay," he said evenly.

She went into the villa and upstairs to her room, feeling depressed. It did not take her long to re-pack the few things she had taken from her bag. The wet bikini she tied up in a plastic bag. She put on a pair of jeans and a thin shirt, brushed out her hair and carried her bag on to the landing. Ricardo was in the hall. Clearly, he had recovered from the shock of her going for he was smiling as he took the stairs two at a time. "I will drive you." She was taken aback for she had expected him to protest.

"That's very kind."

He put her bag in the trunk and opened the passenger door. Claire took a last look around the little creeper-strewn court, at the blaze of purple bougainvillaea, at the scarlet geraniums that fell in luxuriant tails across the top of the garages and down the sides. Suddenly she felt sick with disap-pointment as she climbed back into the car, and painfully let down. Had June heard of her arrival and, unable to face her, run away? Would the man Luiz tell her the truth if she asked him if had telephoned the villa to tell June of her arrival? What would Aunt Marcia and Nancy say to this turn of events? Possibly that Manuel was having an *affaire* with another woman and it was no more than they expected.

The little sports convertible ran out of the drive and turned into the road. Claire's hands were clasped tightly in her lap and in an effort to control her emotions she was looking down at them, biting her lips, so she did not notice that the car turned uphill. When she lifted her head, to her astonishment, she found Ricardo had brought her to the top of the rise behind the villa. A mushroom of pink tiled roofs and green treetops below them showed that the villa was indeed one of a complex, cleverly planned. The town was a pink patch on the edge of the distant sea. "Where are you taking me?" she asked sharply.

"I thought, a day in the mountains. Or, we could go to Granada," Ricardo said conversationally just as though there had been no mention of going to Malaga.

Claire sat back despairingly and closed her eyes. A moment later she felt his hand on hers and he was saying: "I'm sorry, Claire. Truly I am. I would have given anything for this not to have happened. But I can't allow you to run away. Not yet."

She heaved an enormous sigh of resignation. "Of course. I'm not blaming you. I would like to visit Granada, but Ricardo, I am not ready to meet Manuel. I really am not."

"We won't meet him. I'll take you to the Alhambra. It is for the tourists. You know the Alhambra? A Moorish palace and gardens."

"I've read of it. You're very kind. Don't you have to work?" She had asked him this question yesterday.

"For the moment, I have some free time," he replied obscurely.

She gave herself up to the inevitability of the situation. "Okay, let's go to Granada."

It was a wonderful day, cloudless and balmy.

Ricardo put the hood of his little sports car down and the wind sang through their hair, flinging it round their faces, whipping color into their cheeks. They swept through small forests where wild roses grew at the roadside, over rocky ridges, around hairpin bends to the shock of a splash of pink almond blossom on the hillside; down into stony river valleys where the melted snow coming from the hills had turned the water a milky green. The Alhambra was wonderful. They parked the car and wandered through the gardens, sat beside fountains, strolled through the palace admiring the frescoes and stone lions. They lunched at a little restaurant where Ricardo assured her Manuel would never appear, and in the late afternoon they drove back slowly through the mountains and stopped at a bar overlooking the bay. Garlic bunches hung from a cart wheel chained to the rafters and around the walls hung badly painted pictures of the little white houses that clustered around the bays.

Ricardo took her out to the terrace to watch the sun going down. "Have you decided where I'm going to stay tonight?" she asked ruefully, accepting that the matter had been removed from her hands.

"I'm taking you back to the villa. To Manuel."

She had not expected that. "No," she replied, reacting violently. "I will not stay with him."

Ricardo looked distressed. "I live in the town. It isn't suitable for you to be there, too."

"Oh Ricardo, what nonsense. The town's big enough to contain us both. But if it isn't, then take me to Malaga. Or put me on a bus or train. Or, better, give me back my car keys. Or have you had it picked up?" She was so far in his hands now, it would not have surprised her to find the car was gone, that he had had the gentle audacity to get rid of it.

"Yes. The car is gone." He leaned forward and took her hands across the little white table. "If you stay here I can see you every day."

Of course. And that was why she had not tried, really tried, to hold out against him. But her mind was a prey to confusions and she had at least to try to sort things out. "Who is Rosita?" She had meant to ask the question casually but it burst out of her.

"Just a friend. Do you not have men friends in England?"

"Of course." But none, she might have added, who would ask for her in the proprietary manner Rosita had used.

Astonishingly, he seemed to have put her question aside. They drove back down the long hill to the town. "Please, Ricardo, arrange for my car to be brought back."

"It's too late," he told her. "The businesses will be closed."

She bit back her chagrin. "Then perhaps you can tell me how the buses and trains run. It's no use arguing, Ricardo. I will not stay. I don't want to see Manuel until June comes back."

He shrugged resignedly. "All right, you won't stay. So, we will have dinner here, and then I'll drive you to Malaga."

"No. By the time we've finished eating it will be too late to find a hotel."

"I will telephone for a reservation."

She allowed him to win because, clearly, there was to be no other way.

Ricardo parked his car in the square. "I must telephone now. Will you wait here?"

He hurried away. Unable to relax, Claire sat fiddling with her handbag, her thoughts troubled. She wished she knew why Ricardo seemed so unconcerned about June's absence. She wished he would tell her what had been written in the note June left. And she wished, now, confusedly, that she had not enjoyed herself so much today in Ricardo's company. A nun came out of the town shadows and disappeared around the back of the church. A group of men went by looking in at Claire with curiosity. A few moments later Ricardo returned. He was smiling. "It is okay. I have a reservation for you at a very nice hotel."

"You haven't spoken to Manuel?" she asked suspiciously.

"No. I have not spoken to him. Come, we will have something to eat." He took her hand, helping her out of the car.

She had suspected he would call Manuel. Now, feeling certain he was telling the truth, she felt both ashamed and ridiculously happy. Ricardo had lost his windblown look. "You've been to your room and changed," she exclaimed accusingly. She looked down at her jeans and wrinkled blouse. She flicked her windswept hair away from her shoulders. "Now I feel grubby and untidy by comparison with you. I'd like to change before we eat. And have a wash. Is that possible?"

"You will go to my room after all?" He gave her a quizzical look.

"Why not, if you'll carry my bag?" Even as she said it she had a feeling of the trap closing again, but the trap was velvety now, and comfortable. A small voice in the distance, nonetheless, was telling her to run. But something else had taken over. She had to have dinner, didn't she? Against all common sense and reason she said to herself: "It will be all right."

SEVEN

He carried her bag across the square and they entered a tiled and windowless vestibule. There were narrow, tiled stairs. An old woman opened a door and stared at them. Ricardo greeted her with: *"Buenas noches, Señora."* She gave him a chilly glance. He turned to Claire with a wry look.

"Your landlady?"

"Yes."

"I'll be as quick as I can."

They climbed two flights and Ricardo opened a door. It was not a large room but there were long windows opening on to a balcony. The curtains were moving gently in the evening breeze.

Ricardo put Claire's case down on the bed. "I'll go outside and admire the geraniums while you change. There's a bathroom in the hall."

"Thanks." She took out a long, pale pink cotton dress and shook the creases away. It was a new one, flared from the shoulders in the latest style and the soft color suited her. In the bathroom mirror she received a shock. She had not realized how disheveled she was. She washed, brushed her hair and made up her face. When she returned to the bedroom she slipped into the dress, glanced at herself in a mirror and called Ricardo in from the balcony.

"Ah! You are beautiful!" he exclaimed delightedly. "That is new—without a belt? The latest style?"

Claire nodded. "You like it?" She swung in a circle and the skirt flared around her.

"I think it is very pretty indeed." He took her hand and held it high, making a ceremony of crossing the room. "What a pity we are not going dancing."

Suddenly, without warning, the door burst open. Claire swung round, startled, to see a large, handsome woman, her face dark with anger, striding into the room as though it was hers. She had thick black hair drawn severely from her face into a roll across the back of her head, and her fine, flashing eyes were deep set, heavy lidded. When the first shock was over Claire knew immediately who she was for she had that look of immense inner power that was part of Manuel. This must surely be Josefina, the *grande dame* of the family.

"Mama!"

"Ricardo!" And then an explosion of high-pitched Spanish accompanied by furious gesticulations.

Ricardo reacted violently. "Mama!"

Claire, alarmed, backed towards the balcony. Josefina's voice rose, her accusations poured out in a stream. Ricardo, unable to control his mother's fury, put a hand to his forehead in a gesture of despair. Josefina was pointing to Claire's dress, and to her bewilderment, Claire saw that Josefina's face was twisted with anger and disgust. She looked down at the offending garment. It was not particularly bare, not by any means skin tight. Suddenly, to Claire's utter disbelief, Josefina stopped shouting, moved forward, and folded her in her arms. Released, Claire's head was spinning.

Ricardo said sheepishly, trying not to laugh: "I'm sorry, Claire. This is my mother. She speaks no English."

"Doesn't she know I don't speak Spanish?" Claire could see Ricardo was trying hard not to laugh.

"She's a little distraught. My landlady has called her here." Ricardo added apologetically: "My landlady told her I didn't sleep in my room last night. And Manuel has told her you're here in the town, and were with me. So, my mother asked this woman to let her know when I returned."

Claire reacted defensively. "Has anyone told her about Manuel?"

Ricardo said gently: "You must understand it is for you and your reputation that my mother cares."

Another flood of what sounded like accusations came from Ricardo's mother. She was pointing once more at Claire's dress. "What's the matter with what I'm wearing?" Claire asked Ricardo nervously. "She obviously finds this outfit offensive. What on earth's the matter with it?"

Ricardo's smile was strained. "She says you're wearing your nightgown. I've tried to explain it's the new fashion that hasn't reached our town yet, but she won't believe it." Their eyes met and Ricardo's mouth twitched. "Perhaps you would like to show her your nightgown which will be quite dissimilar," suggested Ricardo, diffidently.

Claire said desperately: "I'd do anything to mollify her, but I don't have one. I don't wear them." She choked back a hysterical little laugh. "The ball's in your court."

Ricardo brushed a hand across his mouth as though he could wipe the laughter away, then he was speaking soothingly to his mother. Claire looked down at her dress. To be fair, she thought, it could be a nightdress. There was not all that much difference, these days. Its pale color might be misleading and the fact that there was no belt.

Josefina seemed calmer. Ricardo turned to Claire: "My mother would like you to go to her apartment. To stay with her. She asks me to convey the invitation."

Claire's heart sank. "How can I? We can't communicate at all. It would be a hopeless and impossible situation."

Oddly, Ricardo glanced away. "It would please my mother if you were to go home with her," he said awkwardly. And then he startled Claire by saying: "You must realize you're her beloved Juanita's daughter. She wishes to look after you."

Claire stared at him in disbelief. They were on their way out to dinner! Surely Josefina did not have such control over her grown sons? There was something in Ricardo's manner that reminded her of his brush with Manuel. It was almost as though, she thought, these two people had a hold over him. That trapped sensation was coming over her again. If she could not dine with Ricardo then she had to get away. But what did it mean? There was nothing weak about Ricardo. Thinking about the way he had taken her Hertz car from her, captured her and driven her to Granada today, she thought: In his own way he is a despot, too, though a kind and gentlemanly one. Why does he obey the others, if reluctantly? Why did she have this feeling that everyone watched him? There was the man Pascual who had driven them out of the restaurant. Manuel. And now their mother. She picked up her jeans and shirt, cosmetic bag and hair brush. Josefina had begun once more to issue instructions. In silence Claire packed her belongings into her case. She clipped the locks, then turned, and without looking directly at Ricardo, said: "I think it's better that I take a taxi to Malaga. You stay with your mother."

"Claire, you cannot do that," he protested. "We can't allow you to."

She fought against a desire to try to stay with him. "I'm sorry, Ricardo, but I don't belong to your family. This situation is something I can't cope with. If you'll give me the name of the hotel—"

Ricardo took her hands. "My mother will be very distressed. Please understand that she feels responsible for you."

"Perhaps you'd like to tell her she might have made herself responsible for June's happiness," Claire flashed bitterly.

She saw that hooded look, that quick withdrawal. Then: "My mother loves Juanita,"

Ricardo protested gently. "She loves her very dearly, as a daughter. She would not have this happen for the world."

What was the use? Behind the correctly arranged English words there was no meeting point. She was dealing with something totally beyond her. Claire heaved the case off the bed and headed for the door. "I'll find myself a taxi, and somewhere to stay." She fled through the door and ran down the stairs. There was a pounding of feet and Ricardo caught her up, taking the bag from her. Claire ran ahead two stairs at a time. At the entrance Ricardo caught her up again. She was half-crying. He put an arm around her shoulders. "Come, we will put the bag in the car, then go off and have dinner. I'm sorry it had to happen. You understand my mother is old-fashioned."

It was that old Ricardo again, tossing his problems aside. Was he somehow in their debt? Or, strangely under their jurisdiction? Why was he so lively and confident a man when the two of them were together, and yet polite, careful and willing to obey when in the presence of his family? And then, facing the thing she kept hidden at the back of her mind: Who was Rosita? Why did she feel she had a right to summon him, and why did no one mention her?

Ricardo put her suitcase in his car then they went to a little restaurant facing the sea. "Do we have to sit inside?" Claire asked. The water was calm, the moon rising behind one of the big palms that grew along the waterfront. She felt the need of fresh air and freedom.

"If it's not too cool, we will sit outside," Ricardo agreed. Groups of young men wandered up and down the street, eyeing Claire interestedly, addressing Ricardo cheerily. "There's nothing for them to do in such a small place," Ricardo explained, "except go from bar to bar greeting their friends." The manager came, slapping Ricardo on the back in a friendly fashion.

"Everybody in the town knows you," Claire commented, smiling up at him as the tension in her relaxed. And likes you, she might have added.

"Of course, I grew up here. We all did."

"That's nice."

"Yes. To be part of a whole. Who do you have in England?"

"The aunt, uncle and cousin who looked after me. And some more distant relatives I've never really been in contact with."

"You were lonely," Ricardo said. It was not a question.

"If I was, I was not aware of it. The English prize their independence, you know."

Ricardo made a scoffing sound. "Independence is nothing. It is the family that counts." He ordered paella because Claire had never had it before, and a wine made from grapes grown in the local hills. The food came in a big bowl, mountains of saffron yellow rice piled high. Mussels in their shells lay on top, and below, a delectable mixture of prawns and chicken, beef, squid, fish, vegetables. "This is a rough introduction to the real Spain," Ricardo told her, his blue eyes twinkling. "Paella isn't every foreigner's cup of tea."

"Don't call me a foreigner. I'm English."

He laughed. "I know. I know. Remember I went to an English university. I have an English sister-in-law. I've learned something of your illogical outlook. In Spain you are a foreigner, Miss Claire Richardson, for the very fact that you are English." He served her with a generous helping. "Now try that. Paella used to be a Sunday national dish. Cooks used up the scraps from the week's meals. Now, it's a delicacy in its own right. You'll love it," he told her confidently.

"I'm sure I will." It was becoming increasingly easy to understand how the villa came to be built as a surprise for June. The Manzales women, Claire suspected, would be spoiled to a high degree, so long as they accepted. June's running away was taking on the aspect of a mere gesture to be treated with tolerance—or even amused contempt. Claire thought: Perhaps my mother and I are cut out from the same pattern. Father had me in a trap without my realizing it. Odd, that she had not felt the trap's clamping jaws until after his death.

Suddenly Ricardo surprised her by asking: "Do you know that Juanita remembers your birthday? She is always sad and emotional at such times. We don't mention it, but we all know, and we try to be kind to her."

"Manuel too?"

"Manuel particularly. He feels your loss keenly because, of course, he was the cause of it all."

"I'm getting confused," said Claire. "I expect it's the wine." A moment earlier she had hated Manuel. Had not wanted to meet him again until June returned. Had expected to hate him even then for the way he had belittled Ricardo. For his apparent lack of consideration for June. "Tell me, Ricardo, who sits at the top of the tree when it comes to a test of strength, your mother, or Manuel?"

He seemed amused. "Of course Manuel is the head of the family, but wouldn't any man take advice from an older woman of great experience whom he respected? You don't answer. What are you thinking, Claire?"

She was looking hard at a middle-aged man who was strolling by, his eyes intently on her. Something about him seemed familiar. Then, as he came abreast of them, their eyes met and she recognized the heavy brows, the narrow-eyed look of the man who had wanted to share their table in the bar the night before.

"There's that fellow again, Ricardo. The one who bothered us in the bar."

Whether Ricardo had seen him approach or not she was uncertain. He said without looking up: "Fernando Pascual? Ignore him." The man went on without greeting him. "You were going to tell me what you were thinking about."

She said dryly: "The question was about taking advice from older people. My aunt, whom I love and respect, did not want me to come here. Is that an answer?"

"Perhaps your aunt is not so experienced as my mother who has brought up ten children and had a very hard life."

"There are ten of you! Ten! You mean Manuel supported *nine* brothers and sisters from the age of twenty when his father died?" In a way, she meant: You mean, I have to deal with eight more of you?

"No, there were four babies lost between Manuel and me. That's why there is such a big gap in our ages. He's thirty-nine, I, twenty-seven. My mother has suffered. From this she has acquired great wisdom and very great character. She is a wonderful woman. It's a pity she doesn't speak English. You will have to learn Spanish so you can talk to her."

"Why, since her family speaks English, does she not learn?"

"She does not wish to," Ricardo replied tolerantly.

A little later Claire said: "I've never met anyone like you, Ricardo. You're rather a special person, aren't you?"

"Special person?" He considered, a little amused. "No, I am very ordinary, and besieged by problems like everybody else. Now tell me, what have you decided to do?"

"I still want to go to Malaga."

"Very well, you shall go."

"But I don't want you to have that long drive. I'm quite capable of getting there myself. I'm sure there's a bus or train."

"I shall take you." He called for the bill.

She saw Manuel coming. Half a head taller than the tallest man in the street and with his massive head high like a dark Apollo at war with the years. Claire saw him properly now as she had not seen him the night before. A big, lusty man he was, who walked like a king. He had magnificent side-whiskers and his thick, glossy hair was swept across the tops of his ears to curl into the nape of his neck. She did not draw Ricardo's attention and neither did she get up to run. She knew already that there was an inevitability about Manuel's coming, and perhaps she had known since Josefina folded her so proprietorially in her arms, that there was to be no escape.

EIGHT

It was easy to see how her mother had fallen for him, Claire thought, trying to be fair. He was like a warm southwesterly gale, and as irresistible. "You will love Manuel," Ricardo had said. At the moment she merely felt overwhelmed. And uncomfortable, too; embarrassed by his obvious sexuality. She had wanted to drive to the villa in Ricardo's little sports car, but instead she found herself in the big Mercedes with Manuel at the wheel, crushing her with his warmth. Manuel put a hand over hers on the seat, imprisoning it. Too young for a stepfather, too conscious of his masculinity, he disturbed her.

He was delighted that she had come at last, and he mourned the lost years. He thought she was lovely, with her blonde hair and fair complexion. He told her warmly she was a carbon copy of the girl with whom he had fallen in love. And they would cherish her as their own now that at last the opportunity had arrived. His voice itself was powerful as a mountain torrent with cadences as soft as spring water, his arguments unanswerable. Whatever was in Manuel for women, and Claire recognized with rising nervousness that there was a great deal, it was overflowing and it ran from an apparently inexhaustible spring. Claire saw now the likenesses and the differences between the two brothers. Ricardo, for all his lesser years, had a nobility that Manuel lacked. And though they shared enormous vitality, Ricardo's undoubted fire and strength was overlaid with an air of tranquil confidence that bore no relation to the rude thrust of Manuel's kingship.

Teresa was summoned to the villa to sleep so that the proprieties might be correctly observed. Teresa, too, was twenty-one. Manuel had set her up in a boutique in the town. She was a slim, pretty girl with Ricardo's blue eyes and his gentle manner. It was hard to believe she was the daughter of the ebullient Josefina. She laughed merrily when Claire told her Josefina had mistaken her dress for a nightgown. "She does not follow the fashions. When she was poor there was no point. Now, she is too big."

Claire wanted to ask her another question but dread of the answer held her back. *Would Josefina have behaved so hysterically if she had found me in Leopoldo's room?*

They sat on the verandah looking out into the starlight, talking. It seemed as though nobody ever wanted to go to bed in Spain. Claire told them what she had told Ricardo about her coming and they fired questions at her as they sat over their drinks. "How lonely you must have been," and "how sad, to be without a family."

"I had friends."

"Ah, what are friends? It is the family that counts."

"Manuel," she asked once, "would you really have accepted a two-year-old child when you were twenty? To bring it up as your own, in spite of having six other dependants?"

"But why not? You are a daugher. My English daughter," Manuel kept saying, looking at her with pride, leaning across the space between them and clasping her hand warmly in his. She wanted to tell him he was a mere eighteen when she had been born. That she could not see a man of thirty-nine as a father. But she could not bring herself to say any of these things. Manuel hypnotizes everybody, she thought resentfully. I was half-drunk on the wine or I would not have come.

Claire looked across at Ricardo, his face pale in the light from the wrought-iron lantern hanging above their heads. He smiled back with tenderness and perhaps a touch of triumph. Had he, too, obscurely, won in bringing her back? Footsteps sounded behind them and Manuel turned lazily to look into the dimly-lit house. A young man appeared, tall as Manuel and Ricardo but with a lot of soft fair hair. "I heard Juanita's daughter was here."

"Of course," Manuel replied, smiling with satisfaction. "It's all around the town. Ricardo has been showing her off. Come in, Leopoldo." Leopoldo had brown eyes and an angelic smile. He kissed Claire's hands, then joined the little circle on the verandah. Teresa brought another glass and the family drank to Claire's health. "Leopoldo builds my houses," Manuel was saying. "If you're a property developer it's essential to have an architect and a builder in the family." They all laughed except Ricardo whose face had gone taut. "My little brother is not busy at the moment," Manuel was saying, reaching over to drape a fatherly arm round his youngest brother's shoulders: "He could show you around, Claire."

"I'm sure it's not necessary for him to bother. I'm sure he's busy," she said.

"Oh no. There's no work for Leopoldo at the moment."

"I'm not busy either," Ricardo put in mildly, tapping a cigarette on the table, not looking at them. "I've been showing Claire around today and had no complaints." Through the charged silence a clock struck midnight.

Manuel shifted his great body preparatory to rising. "I have to talk to you, Ricardo," he said. "I'm going down to the town shortly. We'll go together."

Claire, stifling a gasp at the way Manuel was deliberately getting rid of his brother, glanced across the room but Ricardo's expression gave nothing away. Then, all at once he sat up straight, lifted his head and said: "I did put the plans in, if that's what you want to know. They expect to make a decision shortly." There was iron-hard defiance in his tone. Manuel, unmoved, regarded him thoughtfully.

Teresa jumped up, looking disturbed. "I will

get you some more whisky, Manuel. That bottle's empty."

"No," said Manuel, rising and stretching his arms, flexing his shoulders. "It's time we went. You girls will want to go to bed."

"But I haven't talked to Claire," Leopoldo protested. "I've only just arrived."

"It's after midnight. You arrived too late." Manuel cuffed him playfully across the head. "Tomorrow, you will take Claire wherever she wants to go."

Claire stood up precipitously, knocking her empty glass to the floor. By a miracle it did not break. Hiding the outrage she felt behind her hurried movements, she bent to retrieve it. I must be mad, she thought, to let myself in for this. She snatched up Manuel's glass. She did not look at Leopoldo as she hurried out to the kitchen. She put the glasses on the sink. Ricardo entered. He said, quite casually, as though nothing had happened: "Go down to the boutique with Teresa in the morning. That's the best way. I'll see you there. Manuel sleeps late."

"Where's Manuel going now?"

Ricardo made a careless gesture. "Around the bars. He does business that way. He never goes to bed before three. Claire, you're angry."

"Yes," she admitted. "I'm sorry, Ricardo, but I'm not accustomed to being pushed around like this."

He said drily: "It seems to me your father pushed you around, as you say."

"Then there are subtler ways of doing it. I will not be handed to Leopoldo on a platter. Why

Leopoldo? Why does Manuel not want me to associate with you? For that's what it is, isn't it? First your mother, then Manuel."

"And nor will you be handed to anyone on a platter," Ricardo replied soothingly.

"You're ignoring my questions," Claire said sharply.

"It is better that way. There's plenty of time. You're upset. It has been a difficult day."

She was upset, and she knew it. She went out of the door that led into the hall, and straight up to her room. She closed the door and leaned against it, eyes closed. When she had calmed a little she went over to the dressing table and began to brush her hair. A moment later there was a timid knock at the door

"Come in."

Teresa's eyes were wide and she looked faintly distressed. "Manuel and Ricardo are going. They want to say goodnight."

Claire rose, forcing a smile. She went to the head of the stairs. They were standing in the hall. Manuel came up to her and taking her face between both of his hands, kissed her on either cheek. He stood back then, still looking into her eyes, his hands slipping down to her shoulders. "You are not happy, little Claire."

She was not, it was true. "I don't understand why no one is doing anything about finding my mother."

"How can we? She didn't take her car. If she had, we could perhaps have traced the number."

"You could inform the police."

There was a startled silence. Then Manuel said

placatingly: "This is a family affair. We don't want it to be made public."

"I don't mind publicity." She regarded him steadily and he returned her look, his eyes affectionate but faintly puzzled. She glanced down at the upturned faces below.

"But that's because you don't live here," Manuel said with authority. "Juanita wouldn't like it."

"Perhaps it would cure her of running away." No one answered. "How often has it happened?" They stared at her, surprised that she should question Manuel. His hands had slipped down from her shoulders. "This isn't the first time, is it?"

Leopoldo, Teresa and Ricardo stood in a little line at the bottom of the stairs. Their faces, upturned, looked strained.

"Can you tell me how often it's happened? And the reason?" She saw the fire come up behind Manuel's eyes and she could tell by his slow, controlled breathing that he was suddenly angry. That he considered her questions to be impertinent.

"What happens between a husband and wife is not a daughter's affair."

"I think it is, if her mother disappears. You haven't told me how often she has run away."

"I don't think it's important."

"What you don't think is important," said Claire angrily, "is that I should know about my mother. Can't you see I'm worried sick?"

"Oh no. No." Manuel was gently sympathetic. "There is no need. I've told you that. She will return," he said with supreme and monumental confidence.

"Has she got a bank account?" Claire asked. She knew she was treading on dangerous ground, but she did not care.

Manuel was outraged. He turned and with an angry gesture marched down the stairs. "Come, Ricardo. The little Claire will feel calmer in the morning. She has had a long and worrying day." He turned to Teresa. "You will look after her well, Teresa."

Claire stared woodenly after the three men as they went out the door. Then she flashed around to Teresa. "Why should I not ask questions?"

Teresa said unhappily: "Why should Juanita have a bank account of her own? Manuel gives her all the money she wants, and he pays the bills."

"Englishwomen like to be independent."

"Do you think that after nineteen years in Spain Juanita is likely to be thinking like an Englishwoman?"

"Perhaps not. The reason I asked the question was because, without money, my mother can't go far. Hotels are expensive. It seems to me that without money she has to go to friends. And if she is with friends, then she's traceable. All you have to do is telephone the possibles."

"Do you think they would tell?"

"Then drive there, and call unexpectedly. There can't be too many people she would go to. Even if she has a hundred friends, there would be only a small percentage a runaway wife would go to. Manuel must know who those are. Why are you looking at me like that, Teresa? It seems an intelligent enough assumption."

She said uncomfortably: "A man like Manuel does not run after his wife. He would wish for her to return of her own accord."

"Oh *no*! You mean, he is too grand to eat humble pie? That he is such a—a—despot? Oh, the conceit! He expects to hold me here, worrying, because he is too superior to take a step towards getting June back?"

"It is perhaps not quite like that," replied Teresa, looking uncomfortable again. "It may be that he wishes her to come because she wants him. How can he love a woman who does not love him? And he can only be sure she loves him as he loves her if she returns of her own accord."

Claire sighed. "I'm sorry. I'll try to see it his way. But he's so arrogant! Will you tell me how often this happens? June's running away."

"Not at all."

"Why cannot Manuel say that?" When Teresa glanced away she answered it herself, wearily. "I know. He will not be questioned by a mere woman. That's it, isn't it?"

"You must understand that since the age of twenty Manuel has had all the authority. He is not accustomed to being questioned. But that doesn't mean he is a despot, Claire. He would be hurt by your saying that. He is the father of us all and he carries all the problems of the family."

"He wants it this way. He wants to control everyone. Isn't that true?"

"He wishes to have us all together, that is all."

"Then what is this between Manuel and Ricardo? Dare I suggest that Ricardo does not want to be controlled by his elder brother?"

"Ricardo, it is true, wishes to work independently. It is because he does not wish to work on houses all the time. There is trouble at the moment," Teresa admitted, "because Ricardo has made a design for a hospital that is to be built near Malaga."

"That's what he was talking about when he said he had put the plans in?"

"Yes. You see, if Ricardo's plans are accepted he will never work with Manuel again."

"But surely Manuel would be pleased, and proud, if Ricardo made a successful career for himself?"

"He does owe everything he had to Manuel. His education. Everything."

"Owe it?" exclaimed Claire incredulously. "I don't see that he does. Manuel had everything from your father. Everything, Ricardo told me."

"Manuel is the eldest son. It is right."

"Then surely he has the responsibility to look after the others, since they didn't get a share."

"Of course. And he did."

"Surely Manuel doesn't expect you all to become his chattels."

"You don't understand," said Teresa stiffly, turning away. "You are not Spanish. It is late; we must go to bed. One thing, before we part: I have seen the way Ricardo is looking at you, and the way you, well, the way you are not looking at Leopoldo. Don't fall in love with Ricardo, Claire. There could be nothing but unhappiness."

Claire exploded: "Manuel doesn't tell me which of his brothers will take me out. I did not look at Leopoldo because he was handed to me on a platter like a cooked fish, and as Ricardo pointed out, he had already been showing me around. We had become friends."

"That is good. But please," Teresa said, looking sweetly distressed, "do not let it be more than friends."

"Why not? Because he is going to be in trouble with Manuel over these hospital plans, and that could cause a rift between myself and June? Let's get June back," Claire suggested, "before we start worrying about such minor details."

"It is not that."

Claire was turning towards her room. Now she hesitated, her mind spinning back. "Rosita," the name burst out. "Someone called Rosita called. Is she the one you're thinking about?"

"It is because of Rosita," Teresa admitted, "but I don't want to talk about it. Only to warn you. Do not fall in love with Ricardo, or allow him to fall in love with you."

Claire said lightly to hide the disturbance in her: "There's no end to the rules around here. Well, good night. Perhaps I can go down to the boutique with you in the morning. I'm not anxious to sit round here waiting patiently for your big brother to wake up after his late night out."

Teresa followed her to the doorway. "You must understand that is the way Manuel does business. In the bars at night. That is where Spaniards talk."

"Yes. That's what Ricardo told me. But remember what you said before," she found herself adding bitingly. "I'm English and unaccustomed to your Spanish ways. Forgive me if I remain unconvinced." She went into her room, closing the door firmly behind her. Then she sat down at the dressing table and put her head in her hands. Perhaps she should call Aunt Marcia and ask for her advice. But she did not want them telling her how lucky she was that her father had been iron-willed about her custody. That June, at forty-four, was apparently as flighty as she had been at twenty-five. That Claire had better get out of the clutches of this extraordinary foreign family and return home.

She undressed slowly and slipped into bed thinking of Ricardo. The moon had cast a pale golden light across the bedcover. Teresa did not want to talk about this woman Rosita. Was Rosita the real reason for Josefina trying to separate her from Ricardo this evening? For separation, she was certain, was what the scene had been about, over and above the skirmish on morals. Josefina did not want her to be with Ricardo. Why had Manuel tried to hand her over to Leopoldo when Ricardo patently had nothing to do? Rosita again? And yet Ricardo did not mention her. Why? She had never met anyone like Ricardo before. So wise. So kind. So firm. The French had a word for it. *Sympathique*. A strong, defiant man who kept faith with himself, yet bent with the wind when the wind blew too hard. Or so it seemed.

Odd, that Manuel had arrived just as they finished dinner. Could Ricardo have turned fifth columnist and telephoned him?

She switched her thoughts hurriedly away. This was a pretty room and presumably June had decorated it. This was her mother's home and her mother was in some kind of difficulty. I will not go back, she said to herself. Turning over, she buried her face in the pillow. Heaven knows what will come out of this, but I will stay and see it through.

NINE

There was a note on the kitchen table. *Juanita would take much pleasure in introducing Claire to the town.* "But the town knows already," Claire said, laughing derisively. "The barman where I had lunch the day I arrived recognized me."

"That is different," Teresa pointed out. "Manuel means if I actually say, 'This is Juanita's daughter' there will be excitement, and family friends telephoning the villa, and then everyone will want to know where Juanita has gone."

It was understandable that Manuel would, for the moment, like to keep matters at a low key. "Okay. I'm a secret. Now, how will we get to the town?" Claire asked briskly.

"I have a little car. You may borrow it any time you wish."

"How kind." They were all kind. Overwhelmingly so.

The boutique was fun. It was in a short street
that ran from the alleys to the sea and it was full of
cafés that were bright with window boxes, and
tiny shops. Chairs and tables spilled off the
pavement. There were gay striped awnings over
bars and umbrellas shading tables that here and
there overflowed into the sunny street. And it was
a street for pedestrians. Any driver who was
unlucky enough to lose his way, or who foolishly
decided to bring his car to do business here, found
himself ignored. Eyeing the lively muddle
amusedly, Claire could not help wondering what
a stern-faced English traffic warden would make
of it.

The boutique itself was a box with an open
front. Teresa's stock hung from the walls and
flowed out into the street: jeans; jumpers in the
bright Spanish reds and greens that flattered the
Mediterranean coloring; rope-soled sandals;
hand-crocheted shawls from the hill villages;
handmade lace. There were no tourists as yet, and
even in the high season, it seemed, not many of
them came, preferring the excitements of Malaga
and Marbella; or, in the north, Benidorm. Claire
helped lay out the stock but when customers came
in she wandered on to the sea front. Without any
command of the language, there was little she
could do to help Teresa to sell.

It was another cloudless day and beyond,
another empty sea. An airplane flew high
overhead, in the direction of North Africa. She
wandered back down the street, looking at the
fruit stalls with their boxes of bright oranges, the
narrow-doored shops with their jumbled win-

dows and their surprisingly well-equipped interiors. The mother and child who had come to buy a dress were still in Teresa's boutique so Claire sat down outside one of the bars and ordered a coffee. Someone paused beside her, then to her surprise pulled out a chair, scraping it noisily on the stones. Claire's startled eyes flicked upwards. The face with its low brow, the narrow eyes, the heavy features was all too familiar. Pascual.

"*Buenos dias, Señorita.*"

"Do you speak English?" He nodded. "There are many vacant tables," she said in a cool voice. "I would prefer to sit alone."

Pascual nodded insolently, and ignoring her request, seated himself opposite. Claire rose precipitously, but before she had taken a step he said in heavily accented English: "Don't go, Señorita Richardson. I have some news for you."

She had already swung around in the direction of the boutique. Now she swung back. "News? You don't know me. How could you have news for me?"

The waiter appeared. Pascual casually ordered coffee and a cognac. Claire threw a nervous glance towards the boutique. Teresa was still busy with her customers. "You will have an apéritif, Señorita? Another coffee?"

"No, thank you." Could he conceivably know something of her mother's whereabouts? She sat down.

When the waiter had gone the Spaniard said: "I have been watching you and Ricardo."

"Why? Why do you watch us?"

"My name is Fernando Pascual. Does that name mean anything to you?" She shook her head. "You know about Rosita?"

Something cold touched her heart. "No."

"Then it is time someone told you. Rosita is my daughter and Ricardo is to marry her."

Claire, still as a statue, stared sightlessly at the Spaniard. Then, unbelievably, she found herself giving an idiotic little laugh. "I can't see what this has to do with either me or you," she said in a cool voice that she scarcely recognized as her own. "If Ricardo wants to marry your daughter, then I'm sure he will do so."

"It may be that he does not want to, but I am here to tell you that he is obliged to. That is why I warn you to keep away."

"I should think such a reluctant son-in-law was scarcely worth having." Pascual's eyes were like needles and suddenly, under their scrutiny her thin self-possession went. "Obliged?" she echoed.

"No one else will marry my daughter now," said Pascual heavily, "and it is Ricardo's fault that she is this way."

"You mean she is to have a child?"

"I would even wish that to be so. No, it is worse than that. Rosita will never have a child now. She has been in an accident and it was Ricardo's fault. The accident was Ricardo's doing."

Claire's head spun. This was what she had wanted to know. Now the facts were before her she could scarcely believe them. She looked at Pascual in shocked horror. "I am sorry. I am really very sorry, Señor Pascual. This is terrible for you. But Ricardo could not have hurt your daughter deliberately."

The Spaniard shrugged. "Ricardo had a motorcycle. Rosita was forbidden to ride pillion. Then one day he persuaded her to get on it. To save time, I think, for he was going racing and Rosita had to come home. It would have taken too much time to bring her in his car, then return the car to Manuel's villa. They had an accident, and Rosita was very badly hurt. She will never walk again. *And it is Ricardo's fault*," the man repeated harshly. After a little while Pascual said: "You understand, we do not want Ricardo to get involved with another girl when he has this duty to Rosita."

But this was outrageous. "No, I don't understand," replied Claire coldly. "If every man who is involved in an accident with a girl is expected to marry her, then—"

Pascual broke in angrily: "It was not like that. He was going around with Rosita in the daytime as well as the evening. It is not usual in Spain to behave as Ricardo was behaving if a man does not intend to marry a girl. I have seen Ricardo taking your suitcase into his house. You are English and your morals are not my affair, but I can see you are not a street girl and that is why I am warning you. Do not get involved with Ricardo."

"If you'd hung around a little longer," Claire retorted bleakly, "You'd have seen him taking my suitcase out again. I took clothes in because I needed to have a wash and to change. I'm staying with Manuel."

The man's heavy brows lowered over his narrow eyes until the eyes themselves were nearly obscured. "His wife is away."

"Yes."

"You're here to see Juanita?"

"Yes."

"I know where she's gone. I was there, at the villa, just before she left."

With a gasp of astonishment, Claire started forward in her seat. "You? Was it something to do with you?"

"No. I went to see Juanita because Rosita asked me to intervene. To press Ricardo. Some friends came and Juanita left with them. I happen to know who she went away with, and where they live."

"Then please tell me."

His eyes hardened and narrowed. "In exchange for your word that you will not see Ricardo."

"How can I avoid that when I am staying with Manuel?"

"I mean, that you will never have anything to do with Ricardo. It is not necessary, if you are at the villa, to see him. He does not live there. And he should be spending his time with Rosita. You see," said Pascual heavily, "although Ricardo is very, very devoted to Rosita, very much in love with her, there is the problem that there will be no children. This is a bad one. A healthy girl like you could be a great temptation. A man might wish to sacrifice a great love for a family. You understand that in Spain the family is everything," he added, echoing what Ricardo had already told her.

"Would you then wish to inflict a childless marriage on Ricardo? I mean, you're saying you want him for a son-in-law. You must be fond of him. And if so—"

Pascual broke in harshly: "It would be well for you to give me your word. I have it in my power to break Manuel Manzales."

So that was it! Now she understood. Pascual could not force Ricardo to marry his daughter, but his threat was to Manuel. Manuel, the kindly despot who held the family, seemingly, in the palm of his hand. Who issued the orders and expected them to be obeyed. Claire felt herself go cold with something akin to fear. "How dare you threaten me!" She started up, pushing her chair back. "The Manzales are not my concern. I will not be involved in this. If Ricardo loves your daughter then I am sure you have nothing to fear. For me, my interest is in my mother. I would be glad if you would tell me where to find her."

A crafty look came into his eyes. "Not until I have your word that you will not involve yourself with Ricardo."

"I'm afraid I can't be concerned in your affairs," she said, controlling her voice as best she could so that the fear and anger might not show through. "I understand my mother will be back at the weekend to meet the boys from school. I'm sorry about your daughter, Señor Pascual. You have my deepest sympathy, but you can't tie a healthy male against his will to a cripple, whatever you may think his responsibilities are."

"I can break Manuel," Pascual repeated the threat quietly. "And if his brother doesn't marry my little girl, then I will do so."

Claire walked swiftly back to the boutique. Teresa was watching her, her dark eyes worried, her forehead creased into a frown. "Do you already know Señor Pascual?" she asked.

"I do now," Claire replied bleakly. "He's been threatening me. Or rather, he's been threatening Manuel." Teresa turned slightly away. "Tell me,

Teresa," said Claire, looking at the other girl steadily, "as a family, do you really expect Ricardo to marry this girl?"

"Oh dear." Teresa looked distressed.

"You do, don't you?" Claire asked in disbelief. "Does Manuel's dominance really run to forced marriages?"

"Ricardo feels responsible for her," Teresa said unhappily, "and her family expects him to marry her."

"This is what Pascual has been telling me. There was an accident. Ricardo is to blame so he must tie himself to a cripple for the rest of his life! Teresa!"

"Rosita nearly died," said Teresa heavily. "She was a long time in the hospital. Ricardo had been going around with her, it's true, and we all thought he was considering marrying her. The accident brought us together as families. We were suddenly very close, all of us going to the hospital. And all worrying. Fernando started assuming Ricardo would marry his daughter."

"But why, if Ricardo had not actually said so?"

"I don't know. It started slowly. And when a man's daughter is very ill one does not wish to contradict him. Then, when she gets better, it can be too late."

"Is Rosita quite better?"

Teresa nodded. "But she is paralyzed from the waist down. She's in a wheelchair." She hesitated. "The doctors say—"

"What? What do they say, Teresa?" Claire asked sharply.

"That perhaps she does not try hard enough.

With this sort of paralysis—where the spine and therefore the nervous system is involved, a person who wants badly to get better can often do a great deal for herself. I do not want to be hard on Rosita," said Teresa unhappily, "but sometimes one feels she is using her affliction to get sympathy, and to force people to do what she wants. She was always good at getting her own way."

"Manuel and Juanita want him to marry this girl?" Claire asked in disbelief.

"No." Teresa shook her head emphatically. "They do not. But—" she shrugged. "It's a very unpleasant mess, as you would say."

So this was why Manuel and Josefina were trying to keep Ricardo and herself apart! No wonder Ricardo ran to the farm when his problems got on top of him. He had, indeed, problems enough. Appalled, Claire asked: "Was it his fault, the accident to the girl?"

Teresa shook her head. "It was the truck driver's fault. And it was Rosita's fault that she was on the pillion. Manuel had forbidden Ricardo to take anyone for a ride that way. Ricardo tried hard to dissuade her, but you do not know Rosita. When she makes up her mind . . ." Teresa clicked her tongue and shook her head. "Ricardo does not say this in public because of what happened, but he told me that day Rosita was at her most beastly, and to avoid a scene he took her, against his own wishes, and against Manuel's orders."

"She is not a nice girl?"

Teresa shook her head. "Rosita was never a nice

girl," she replied. "Now she has had all this attention she is abominable. I feel very sorry for poor Ricardo."

"Is he in love with her?"

"He will not say he is not because he is very honorable."

Claire walked out of the boutique and down the street to the sea. She sat down on the low stone wall with her legs hanging over the edge, staring unhappily out across the water. She had not told Teresa that Pascual had given her an opportunity to find her mother. It was a decision she had to make on her own. And now she had to make another decision, whether to believe Pascual when he said Ricardo was deeply in love with Rosita and could only be attracted by another woman's healthy body. Something intangible had sprung up between Ricardo and herself. Something she had never experienced with another man. Leaving aside his undoubted attraction, there had been a sort of instant recognition that first day. An affinity that comes normally from a long friendship. But if Manuel was right in his conceit that June would return of her own free will, then there was no need to make any promises to this sinister little man. She heard light footsteps behind her and turned.

"Come," said Teresa, "it's time to go to lunch."

"What do you do? Do you return to the villa?"

"There would not be any lunch at the villa, with Juanita away. Manuel will come down into the town. I am to take you to my mother's apartment.'

"No!" cried Claire almost violently. The thought of facing up to the overpowering Josefina was as bad as the thought of facing up to Manuel.

Manuel! Now that she knew what he was trying to do to Ricardo, she scarcely knew how she would face him.

Teresa looked troubled. "The boutique is closed now until four. It is one o'clock. What do you wish to do?"

"You offered me your car this morning. If that offer still stands, I would like to drive off by myself and think."

"But you must have some lunch."

"I will. Please thank your mother. I'm sure she will understand that I have problems on my mind. What time shall I pick you up?"

"You will need a rest, Claire. It was very late when we went to bed this morning," Teresa said concernedly.

"I will sleep tonight," she replied, taking the car keys from Teresa's reluctant hand. "I'm not accustomed to a siesta. If I went to sleep I would have difficulty in waking up again."

They parted and Claire went unhappily into the square. Teresa's little Fiat was parked under a palm tree close by the church. She walked towards it, hesitated. Something had been niggling at the back of her mind ever since Pascual delivered his threat. She had to think about it now. She stood under the trees, her mind in a turmoil. Was this why June had run away? Because she could not bear to see Manuel do this dreadful thing to Ricardo?

A young man, handsome, in his mid-twenties came up to her and stopped. He spoke to her enticingly in Spanish. Irritated. she pushed past him and seeing the church door open, went up the steps. She needed to think. To calm herself. She did not want to get into the car and drive before she had come to terms with this new dilemma.

It was a big church, and bare. Low wooden chairs with wicker seats stood row upon row in a great block that ran right up to the pulpit. There were perhaps a dozen people, some elderly men and several women in black veils, sitting with heads bowed, or kneeling. Claire stood looking at the ornate altar lit by a shaft from a stained glass window. And then a new thought struck her. A new dimension. I wonder if they made my mother—my Spanish mother Juanita Manzales, into a Catholic, too? June Richardson of England seemed very far away.

She did not hear Ricardo's soft footsteps. She felt his touch on her arm and knew it was him. She turned, looking miserably up into his clever, thoughtful, gentle face, his incredibly blue eyes. "I've been waiting for you," he said.

TEN

There were two boys crossing the square. They greeted Ricardo, turned an interested look on Claire. Ricardo spoke to them in Spanish and they nodded. He tossed Teresa's car keys to them. "They'll take them to the boutique when it opens," he said.

Claire smiled. "You know the whole town."

"And the whole town knows me. There are advantages and disadvantages, I assure you."

They drove past the high-rise apartments and into the hills. Ricardo pulled up outside a bar that was balanced apparently precariously over a small ravine on the outskirts of a village. There were geraniums in wooden vats; a riot of red and yellow flowered begonias; creeping green things.

"Come," he said, taking Claire's hand, "we will have lunch on the terrace here."

The view down the deep valley was breathtaking. Far in the distance on a sea like sheet silver, two fishing boats sat like tiny toys. Above, steep, rocky ridges built one upon the other. Near at hand a small gray donkey munched contentedly, and a hundred yards away a flock of caramel colored goats were nosing briskly at some rough bushes.

"Ricardo, why are you so free?" Claire asked the questions that had been puzzling her. "Why is Leopoldo so free? Isn't there any work to do?"

"No. There is nothing. No building for Leopoldo. And nothing I can do for Manuel at the moment. He's short of cash, that's his problem. Until he sells the hotel he's built, on spec or some of his houses, he can't expand. Besides," Ricardo added firmly, "I do not wish to work for Manuel."

She put her elbows on the table and looked up into his face. She wanted most desperately to ask about Rosita, but something held her back. The waiter came and Ricardo ordered two Campari sodas. Then he turned back to Claire. His eyes were glowing, his facial muscles tense so that the high cheekbones stood out.

"My dream is for my plans for this hospital to be accepted."

She could see now how much it meant to him. Even talking about it there was controlled excitement, anticipation even, in his voice.

"I do hope they are. I wish you luck with all my heart. But if they're not?"

Ricardo shrugged. "Then I shall start up in Malaga. There are jobs to be had in established architectural firms. I shall not be able to afford to buy a partnership." He spoke like a man, if not without problems, then at least without problems that were insuperable. "Let's not talk about me, though. What are you going to do now? Can I persuade you to stay?"

"You must understand that I won't be anyone's prisoner."

"Yes. I understand. But it's only two days until the weekend. Could you not stay until then?"

"In case June returns for Juan and Vicente? I'm sorry, Ricardo, but I can't. I will return if she returns."

He accepted her decision, regretfully. They ate lunch looking down over the valley with the hot sun on their arms. Already Claire had a faint tan, and the heat was relaxing the tensions in her. Afterwards, they drove slowly back to Manuel's villa. There was another maid whom Claire had not seen before. "Tomasa and Oliva take turns during the week when the boys are away, but they both come at weekends," Ricardo explained. He did not seem at all concerned that this woman would tell Manuel it was he who helped Claire with her getaway. Did he, perhaps defiantly, want them to know?

She placed a note on the table where Manuel had left his orders to Teresa that morning. It was brief and to the point. *I am going to Malaga and will be in touch on the weekend.*

Ricardo carried her suitcase out to the car. It was late afternoon by the time they were racing down the coast road, whirling round hairpin bends then bursting out of a mountain fold to a glittering, rock-edged sea, leaping over the tops of promontories with Claire's hair flying in the breeze, diving down into valleys where the road ran close by beaches and the shallow water crept up like green veils across the stones. Ricardo took her to the hotel to book in, then she went with him to the boys' school to leave a message that Claire was here in case June should turn up early to whisk her children away. They went through a big wrought-iron gate as tall as the shiny leafed trees that formed a hedge of sorts on either side, and across a dusty, graveled courtyard. Ricardo rang the bell. A smart maid answered and he was ushered inside. A few minutes later he was back, looking disturbed. He climbed into the driver's seat and reached for Claire's hand. "Don't run away, Claire. Juanita will come back next weekend."

"Next weekend?" Her heart sank. "You were very confident that she'd be back on Friday."

"She sent a message."

"Then I shall stay in Malaga until she comes."

Ricardo accepted that, again regretfully. The shops were starting to open after the siesta. They wandered in and out of the little arcades and streets. She bought a postcard to send home. It showed a flowered patio reminiscent of Manuel's villa. Ricardo knew where to find the handcraft shops and the leather boutiques. He showed her coats of pale leather soft as a lady's glove, and long, elegant boots. Seeing a pair of flat-soled, gold leather sandals covered with tiny flowers Claire gave an exclamation of delight.

"You like those?" Ricardo said. "You have pretty feet. You must have them." He thrust one hand in his trouser pocket. "I will buy them for you."

She protested, but it was no use. Ricardo bought the sandals. The assistant put them in a gloriously gift-wrapped box and Ricardo presented them to Claire with a small bow. So this is the way June lives, Claire thought, feeling warm, and pampered, and in a new way, loved. No wonder she left my father. She would never have had this, as I never had it, from him. She thanked Ricardo delightedly.

"Why are you smiling?"

"Because I am happy." She was also amused, and intrigued, thinking it was not a gesture one would expect from an out-of-work Englishman. They wandered back towards the sea, hand-in-hand. It seemed the most natural thing in the world. They found a little bar with tables scattered on the pavement and sat there sipping sherry as the sun went down. They dined late, then walked back to Claire's hotel at midnight, still hand-in-hand.

"I'll come and take you out tomorrow."

She thought of Rosita, Pascual and Manuel as Ricardo kissed her gently on the lips. *I could break Manuel*, Pascual had said. *And if his brother doesn't marry my little girl, I will do so.* She shivered and Ricardo looked concernedly into her eyes. She put her arms up round his neck and kissed him again, wanting to hide her face, wanting to hide even from herself.

Gently, he released her. "I'll be here about ten." Again that assumption that she would do what he wanted, but perhaps it was only because he knew she wanted it too. That she was irretrievably under his spell.

* * * *

The next morning, Claire wrote her postcard.

> *Dear Aunt Marcia, Uncle Ben and Nancy,*
> *You will no doubt be astonished to hear*
> *that June has two maids, a swimming pool*
> *and a couple of sons. Will keep in touch. Love,*
> *Claire.*

What a silly thing to write! She began to tear the card up, then hesitated. After all, she thought abrasively, was this not what Marcia and Nancy needed to know? Weren't they worried that June's rejected daughter was going to give her inheritance to this undeserving but poverty-stricken runaway? Though there was a box in the hotel, Claire walked to the post office, savoring her freedom. At nine o'clock in the morning the narrow streets were already busy.

She followed a tide of women with shopping baskets and there was the market, overflowing with life and noisy as a hen coop. There were wet tiled stalls smelling strongly of the sea. Small dark men in huge aprons shouting their wares; the slap of wet fish on slabs, the slosh of boots on the dripping stone floor, the rank smell of it. There were clean little butchers' stalls with rolls of beef and veal prettily tied up with bands of fat like thin silk; fruit stalls overflowing with market greens. She loved the blousy red and yellow peppers that one seldom saw at home. There were tiny cheese stalls, all white and gold, and women calling uninhibitedly to each other and to the stall holders.

Claire looked at her watch. "Ten o'clock!" She turned and ran. Ricardo's car was parked at the entrance to the hotel and Ricardo was standing in the entrance, hands in pockets, frowning. He ran down the steps to greet her. "I was worried that you'd run off." He took her hands, raising them to his lips.

"I went to post a card to my relatives and found myself in the market."

"Ah, yes. Everyone loves the market. Come."

She pulled a bright silk scarf out of her bag and tied it over her hair. "Where are we going?"

"I want to take you up into the valleys and the woods, to pick wild flowers and paddle in the streams. And to see the famous bull ring at Ronda, and the gorge where we did frightful things to each other in the Civil War. Do you want to be a tourist?"

"Very much." She smiled delightedly.

"And I will be a tourist guide." They jumped into the car, companionable, happy. And this time Claire did not think of Pascual or Rosita or Manuel at all.

It was a wonderful, magical day. They came back down through the mountains as the moon was rising and had dinner at a little restaurant on the outskirts of the town. Ricardo took her back to the hotel. "I cannot come to Malaga tomorrow."

Claire, waiting for his reason, knowing he had no work to do, waited in vain. Feeling faintly dashed, and desperately disappointed, she said: "That's all right. I'll explore. There's so much to see." She went up the stairs with dragging feet, wondering if he was indeed going to see Rosita. Wondering what it all meant. Wondering about herself. She now had a week to put in before there was any chance of seeing June.

The next morning, wandering through the streets of the town she saw some placards outside a tourist bureau.

"You want day tour?" asked a black-eyed, black-haired boy standing in the doorway with a sheaf of pamphlets in his hand. "Alicanta, Granada, Algeciras, Tangier, scenic mountain ride?" She took a pamphlet and examined it, but she had not the heart to make arrangements to set out on a journey alone. Feeling a little lost, she bought a pair of soft leather gloves for Aunt Marcia and a lizard skin purse for Nancy. For her Uncle Ben she bought a crocodile skin belt. She tried to interest herself in some pictures of the rock-strewn countryside with its harsh lines and square white houses, its startling shadows and blinding sunlight. She wandered down to the waterfront and took a ride in a decorated carriage drawn by a thin horse in a pretty hat. She bought some sweets that proved too sickly to eat.

Why had Ricardo not said he would come again? The more she considered his silence, the more confused she became. Had he decided to give up the fight? Or, less inexplicably, was he a man who did not make promises he might be unable to keep?

At siesta time when the shops closed and the town went dead, she returned to her hotel. The room looked bleak with the shutters closed against the sunlight. She flung them open. Why had she not thought to buy a paperback? The telephone rang. She picked up the receiver, excitement flooding through her. Who could it be but Ricardo, for no one else knew she was here?

"Señor Manzales is here to see you," said the voice from the desk downstairs.

"Thank you. I'll come." She whipped a comb out of her handbag and slid it through her hair; touched her mouth with lipstick. In the mirror her eyes were shining. I should have known Ricardo would come. She hurried to the door, her spirits high as the sky. Because she had been so lonely, the inrush of joy was all the more heady. She pressed the elevator button again and again, impatiently willing it to come.

The door opened and Manuel stepped out. Claire looked at him in shocked silence, the world shrinking round her while Manuel grew, a giant of a man who seemed to overpower her with his personality and his unacceptable, potent sexuality. "You do not mind if I come up? It is to carry your bag," he said in his very precise, tutored English. "You have it ready?"

Was this why Ricardo had not come? Because he had seen what he must do, returned to Rosita yet inexplicably given her away to Manuel so that she would be brought back? Claire felt her face close, her nerves tighten. She would accept Rosita, because she must, but: "I'm not returning to the villa with you, Manuel," she said, "and there's nothing you can do to make me. How did you know where to find me?"

"But of course you are to meet the children," he said with unanswerable authority, ignoring her question. "I'm on my way to the school to collect your little brothers. You do not want to meet them?" he asked, regarding her enquiringly. "Oh no, little Claire, it isn't possible that you could be uninterested in your own blood relations. Come," He held out one hand for her key, and with the other gave her a firm but gentle push.

She felt herself going, and even, as though hypnotized, relinquishing the key. She tried to say she did not want to meet the boys until their mother returned. But was that true? As Manuel said, they were her blood relations, and had she not discovered herself to be very much alone? Manuel said, as they went back into the room: "The children will be glad to have you. A sister will be a great excitement for them and it will cover the disappointment of their mother being away."

"Have you made any attempt to find my mother?" she asked, thinking obsessively of Rosita, trying to convince herself that it was right Ricardo should go to the crippled girl.

"Juanita will come home soon," said Manuel with quiet confidence. "A little time has to pass, you must understand. It's possible to lead people sometimes, but it is not possible to drive them. And there has to be time for a running down of problems and emotions. It is often necessary for time to soften the will, just as it softens grief and anger. You are young, little Claire. And you have not much experience of family."

Numbly, she put the clothes she had unpacked back into her suitcase. She had tried to run away but she had not run hard enough or fast enough because she had not wanted to escape Ricardo, and Ricardo was an integral part of the family, so the ensnarement was inevitable.

"I have paid your bill," said Manuel kindly.

"It wasn't necessary. I must tell you that my father left me well provided for."

"That is good." Manuel picked up her bag. They went downstairs in silence. The big Mercedes was waiting outside. Manuel put her bag in the trunk then courteously opened the door for her and she slid into the enveloping comfort of the front seat.

She said: "Do the boys know I exist?"

"Of course. How could they not?"

Unanswerable. She was left not understanding.

The big gates of the school were open today. The car purred through into the courtyard. Claire could see a group of boys chattering together in the big tiled hall. Two of them broke away and ran towards the door. A man appeared, nodded to Manuel, then returned inside. The boys dashed out. Claire was looking at the boys who were her half-brothers and her eyes were wide with disbelief. She could have been looking at two English schoolboys. They were both tall for their ages, and thin as matchsticks. She had an impression of floppy fair hair falling across broad foreheads, a coltish legginess and suits that hung slack over frail bodies. Then, as they approached she saw that their eyes were that startling blue of Ricardo's eyes, and they had their faintly olive skin from Manuel. They came like a couple of whirlwinds, rushing at Manuel with arms outstretched as no English schoolboy would be likely to come, and Manuel embraced them in turn, kissing each of them on both cheeks, cuffing them affectionately as he might cuff a puppy. Claire had slid out of her seat. She stood in the drive in silence, torn by a mixture of emotions. Manuel turned.

"Juan, my son, this is your big sister Claire," he said in the manner of offering him a box of sweets. "Claire has come from England to visit us."

Momentarily, both boys stared, then Juan stepped forward, held out his hand and raised her fingers gravely to his lips.

"Vicente," said Manuel. The younger boy followed suit. There was almost a military precision about their politeness.

"You look like our mother," said Vicente gravely, then turning to Manuel: "Where is Mama?"

Manuel was hustling them firmly into the back seat. "Your mother is not to be with us this weekend," he said, "she has had to go away."

Claire, climbing back in, felt the silence. She looked back and saw their faces, saw the bitter disappointment, then suspicion sharpening their blue eyes. "Has she gone because Claire has come to stay?" Juan asked bluntly.

"Of course not," interposed Claire, turning smilingly to look at them. "She went before I arrived, but she will be back soon. I am to look after you." These children were not like English children after all. What English boy of fourteen would be so vulnerable to hurt simply because his mother was not there to greet him? As the car purred away, the silence from the back seat grew intense. Even Manuel seemed unable to overcome it, or perhaps he was simply concerned with the traffic. The big car ran through the town. Juan made a sharp, explosive remark in Spanish, and Manuel returned firmly: "It is necessary to speak

English at all times. Your sister does not speak
Spanish."

But the words were not to be stemmed and they
came in a flood, accusative, enquiring, angry. If
Claire could not understand their meaning, she
took the sense well enough. Looking straight
ahead, feeling uncomfortable, she was appalled
when she thought she detected tears in Vicente's
voice. Manuel said, speaking both calmly and
gently: "There can be no answer to anything
spoken in Spanish. One does not speak before a
guest in what is a foreign tongue to her." Claire
turned around to address them, but their closed
faces silenced her and she turned back with a
sinking heart to look at the road.

ELEVEN

All the way up the coast it was the same. Manuel spoke to them calmly and kindly and they replied in Spanish, vociferously at times, and at times sullenly. Manuel carefully forebore to speak to Claire alone. He talked in generalities, including them all, but his kindly words were met with silence or rancor. Claire tried. She sat sideways, with one arm along the back of the seat, and smiling into their wooden faces, told them how she had come to Spain. Only: "My father has died" brought a response. Juan said formally: "We are sorry," after which Vicente butted in tearfully: "That is no reason to drive our mother away."

"I have not done that. How could I do that?" And then, persuasively: "She has to have a little vacation some time, you know."

"She doesn't," retorted Vincente at once childish and rude.

Manuel said: "If you cannot be sensible and courteous, then it's better not to speak at all." After that there was silence for the rest of the journey. Claire sat through it with a heavy heart.

At the villa Juan politely took her case and carried it upstairs, then with a formal little bow that would have been more suited to a hotel porter administering to a grandee, he disappeared. She heard raised voices in the kitchen, the boys and possibly the maid. They went on for a long time, then heavy footsteps came from the hall and Manuel was calmly silencing them. They rushed upstairs and almost immediately down. She saw them racing across the lawn in swimming trunks. Claire put on a bikini and went to join them.

They had been shouting and splashing, working off the explosive element in them. They did not see her, or so she thought, as she approached, but as she dived in they made for the side and sat with closed faces, watching her. "Why don't we have a race?" she asked brightly.

"We don't care to race," replied Juan. "Besides, I have some work to do." They walked back across the lawn side by side, leaving Claire with the sick and angry feeling that she had driven them away. She swam up and down for a while then Manuel came to join her. In his swimming trunks he was a brown giant. He flexed his muscles, threw up his head and took long, exultant breaths of the scented air. Like a bull at pasture, she thought, feeling faintly embarrassed again.

He dived in and swam fast to the other end, then back, his strokes clean and powerful as she had known they would be. She said lightly: "Ricardo says it's too early to swim."

He flung the water from his hair. "Don't listen to Ricardo." And then he was off again, up and down as though he, like the boys, must shed some of his excessive strength and energy.

The maid brought tea and set it under a blue umbrella. Manuel said lightly: "The English cannot live without tea. I will accompany you with a glass of whisky because tea is bad for my stomach."

"Really?"

"Oh yes. I think it would be. That's why I've never tried it." She laughed, liking him briefly, feeling a little more at home with him. "The boys are not coming to join us," he added. "They're working on Juan's Vespa which probably has nothing the matter with it, but it is good for Juan to know how an engine works. He spends as much time taking it to pieces as he does riding it. Juanita doesn't like him to have it. She would shield the children from all danger, but that is wrong. It is a dangerous world, and they must learn to cope with it early." The telephone rang. The maid came out to call Manuel. Afterwards he came back across the lawn unhurriedly, his head high as though he walked before a hundred pairs of eyes. He was carrying a terrycloth robe and Claire, taking it from him, flushed scarlet, realizing that she should have remembered not to sit around so briefly clad; she was annoyed with herself for her discourtesy, and at the same time annoyed with Manuel for his idiotic, old-fashioned standards. A moment later Ricardo and Leopoldo crossed the verandah.

Ricardo! Excitement welled up in her as it always did when he appeared. So! Manuel brought the robe because he had heard the sound of an engine! She bit back an explosion of laughter and tried to stifle consuming delight.

The two men strode across the lawn: one lively, dark and with a swing in his step, the other large as Manuel but without the air of kingship, and fair as Manuel's sons. He greeted them both with affection. A moment later he was saying: "Ricardo, Rosita has been calling for you. She has been bothering our mother and sisters. Could you not find time to go and see her?"

Were his words for Claire's benefit? She could not tell. She was thinking with a new sort of triumph that Rosita was not, after all, the cause of Ricardo's saying he would be unable to see her today. But had he known she would come back? Had he given Manuel the address of the hotel?

Ricardo said casually: "I've been busy." He bent down and kissed Claire's hand formally, so that no one would guess how he had kissed her the day before. Leopoldo followed suit. "Ah! We have missed the ritual of tea," Ricardo said. "I will ask Tomasa to bring some more."

"You are a convert?" Claire asked. Happiness was flowing though her.

"Yes, Juanita converted me to tea when I was not ten years old. I understand it's very bad for the liver but one must drink something and that whisky of yours, Manuel, is bad for the liver too. And so is coffee. If I die this way it will be with the pleasant memories of tea parties with Juanita and that will not be a bad death." He walked off towards the house. Claire laughed delightedly.

Manuel, watching her happiness, frowned. "You would like to take Claire out to dinner tonight, Leopoldo?" he suggested. His voice was abrupt, dictatorial.

Leopoldo nodded shyly. Claire glanced away to hide her anger. Manuel had put his question too cleverly during the odd moment when Ricardo was missing. She said, summoning up a cool voice: "I don't need to go out to dinner. I had a good lunch. I'd like to stay here and look after the boys."

"Ricardo must dine with Rosita," said Manuel, not pointedly at all, not thrustingly, but with the air of putting something to the test. Claire rose, a prey to the torment of emotions that were out of control. She went over to the wall, looking across to the almond blossom on the hillside. Coming here on the plane she had said to herself that this could be the most wonderful summer of her life. The beauty of her surroundings, touching the supreme agony in her throat, brought tears to her eyes. Of course Ricardo must dine with Rosita. She would surmount this dreadful feeling of deprivation: of a love doomed. She would face the fact that her breathless dream of summer had another side. She turned as he came across the grass. He looked so handsome, so young and in an odd way vulnerable. Perhaps it was this vulnerability as much as his lightness of figure and movement that cast off some of the essential resemblance he bore to Manuel. He came up to her and she found herself exploding:

"Manuel says I must dine with Leopoldo tonight." It sounded childish, like telling tales, and even as she said it she was ashamed, and doubly ashamed that Manuel and Leopoldo should inevitably overhear.

Ricardo said serenely: "Then I'm afraid you'll have to dine with me also, because Leopoldo and I are to dine together." She felt her eyes drawn guiltily, obsessively, to Leopoldo.

Leopoldo said mildly, "We can go together." Clearly he did not have the sensitivity of his brothers and perhaps this family drama was not bothering him.

Manuel drained his whisky. He rose. It was impossible to read anything in his face. He went over to the verandah where he had left the whisky bottle and ice bucket. Removing the cork, he turned. "Then let us all dine together," he suggested, his eyes hooded, his face calm. But there was the look of an animal about him now. It was in the way he stood, as though ready to strike. He called through to the house in Spanish and the woman Tomasa appeared. There was a discussion. Then: "Tomasa must go home," he said, "but she says Oliva will be pleased to come. We do not like to leave the boys alone, though they are very independent and would prefer it."

It was not a victory for anybody. Happiness seemed drowned in guilt. Manuel's disapproval hung over them like a cloud.

* * * *

In any event, there was no dinner party, for Juan, eating his supper in the kitchen, was suddenly very ill. That the illness was real there was no doubt, but its origins might have been more obscure. It had happened to Claire in moments of stress. She had been ill on the morning of her father's funeral and Aunt Marcia had said: "What on earth did you eat last night?" But she had had no dinner at all and the disturbance in her stomach had come from her heart and nerves. Juan was put to bed. Vicente, imprisoning himself in his own bedroom with his transistor radio and books, occasionally emerged to sympathize with his brother. Manuel was patently worried. He had stopped trying to make the boys speak English. There seemed little point since Oliva the maid, disturbed by the new state of affairs, was shouting noisily through the house in strident Spanish and Vicente was calling down the stairs to her. Leopoldo had disappeared. Claire rummaged in the enormous refrigerator and found some steak and salad. A while ago she had been hungry. Now, her appetite had gone. She went upstairs to ask Vicente if he wanted anything but he only looked at her with smoldering eyes and said woundingly: "It's all your fault." Of course she should never have given in to Manuel. Of course she should not be here.

After supper, when they returned to the verandah again Manuel took the chair, deliberately, she thought, between herself and Ricardo. She glanced up and met Ricardo's amused eyes. The tug of attraction between them seemed to have grown stronger as she waited for the problems of the family to drive them away.

"Get some brandy, Ricardo, will you?" Though Manuel's words were autocratic, he had a soft manner of delivery that precluded offence. Ricardo went through to the drawing room. Suspecting that Manuel may have sent him off in order to have a private word with her, Claire brought out the brochure that had been given her at the tourist bureau and studied it. In the event, to her relief, Manuel did not speak and as Ricardo returned she tossed the brochure into the waste-paper basket.

Vicente appeared looking small and frail in his pajamas. Manuel took the child on his knee and he snuggled close, his face hidden in Manuel's shoulder. When he spoke it was in Spanish, and Manuel now spoke Spanish, softly, in return.

Claire asked: "Aren't you going to call a doctor for Juan?"

"I don't think so," returned Manuel. "We will see how he is tomorrow. Oliva thinks it is hysteria." He carried Vicente upstairs.

As he went out of the room Claire turned to Ricardo. Looking into his vital yet tranquil face she could see no embarrassment, no guilt. "You told Manuel where I was staying." It was scarcely an accusation for they were together again and she could not blame him, for she had wanted this too.

"He knew I had taken you away. It was necessary to tell." Manuel's wrath, presumably, was something better avoided. But he need not have known, she thought. Oliva need not have seen Ricardo here if he had not wished her to tell tales. But of course they all wanted me. Ricardo, this time, in a family sense. He would think, like Manuel, that I should meet the boys.

Ricardo said: "I'm glad you're back."

"I'm glad, too." They sat in companionable silence until Manuel returned. He came slowly, looking down at them, somehow aware of their happiness. He said heavily: "The boys seem to be settled. Oliva has agreed to stay the night. She wishes to go to bed. We must talk, Ricardo." Claire rose. "You do not have to retire," said

Manuel. "Ricardo and I will go down to the town."

"I'm quite happy to go to bed. It's late."

Ricardo also had risen. Manuel went through to the hall. "Really," said Claire, her voice unintentionally sharp, "I don't wish to drive you away. I'm happy to—"

Ricardo laid a hand on her arm. "You know Manuel does all his talking in bars. We would be going anyway." He kissed Claire's hand, then while Manuel's back was turned, pressed her fingers to his lips.

When they had gone Claire stood alone in the hall, looking at the family photographs. She wandered from one idyllic mother-and-child picture to another, troubled by her own confused reactions. Were these rather showy symbols of successful motherhood spread around to counteract a guilty conscience regarding the child who had been abandoned for the lover?

She went slowly upstairs, leaving the lights on. Manuel, presumably, would be back later. Was she, by providing temptation for Ricardo, holding up this diabolical marriage? But was she providing, also, as Pascual had suggested, merely the understandable temptation of a healthy body? There was the disturbing thought of her likeness to June whom Ricardo obviously loved. Claire paused on the landing. Vicente's bedroom door was open and she could see his face on the pillow, angelic and still in the pale moonlight shafting in from the window. She tiptoed in and lifted the sheet gently away. His face was very pale, the eyes dark-ringed. How much damage, she wondered unhappily, would even a psychosomatic illness do to a very sensitive boy?

Emotionally disturbed, she lingered in the hall, then knowing she would not sleep, wandered back downstairs. The golden hands of the grandfather clock were turned to midnight. She went compulsively back to the photographs. June arm in arm with Manuel. June with a new baby. June hand in hand with two little boys. The likeness to herself was extraordinary. Why had she not told Manuel that Pascual knew where June had gone? Even as she asked herself the question she knew the answer. She could not explain that Pascual had asked her to promise not to see Ricardo. And again, was Pascual right when he said Ricardo really loved Rosita but could be tempted by another girl's healthy body? What kind of misery was she going to store up for herself and everybody else if she encouraged Ricardo?

She was at her most vulnerable when the telephone on the small table by the sofa, shrilled in her ear. She jumped, then picked up the receiver swiftly lest it should disturb the boys and because, for one crazy moment, she thought it might be June.

It was a man's voice. "So, that is the English girl?" She knew immediately and with consternation it was Pascual. "I am looking for Ricardo. Perhaps he is there with you?"

"No," she retorted sharply. "He is not."

"Then where is he?" the man demanded ungraciously. "I have been looking for him all the day. I have telephoned everyone. He must have got my messages." Was that the telephone call Manuel had received? And had he taken Ricardo off to a bar to discuss this very situation? "My little girl is pining because he does not visit her," Pascual was saying. "This is not to be allowed."

"I don't know about Ricardo," Claire replied uneasily. Pascual sounded as though he had been drinking. She guessed he had been searching the bars. Perhaps he was even now telephoning from a bar and would therefore shortly encounter Ricardo and Manuel.

"I think you do know," Pascual retorted, blustering. "It was not like this before you came." His harsh, uncontrolled voice softened a little. "Perhaps you have thought about my offer. You have come here to visit your mother, and your mother has gone. She would be very upset if she knew you could find her but did nothing about it." And surely that was true, Claire thought, suddenly distressed. "You would like her address?"

Mistrusting him, yet inevitably tugged emotionally in all directions, Claire thought of the boys upstairs who anyway would not accept her until June's return. She thought with apprehension of Manuel and Ricardo even now discussing this very situation down in the town. "You know, perhaps," went on Pascual, "that Manuel has had offers for one of his houses? And for the hotel?"

"I don't know about Manuel's business."

"I told you I can ruin him," Pascual's voice was cold, vindictive. "No one will buy any of the houses, or the hotel, if they are not to have access to water."

"What do you mean?"

"I have the only water in the town on my property."

But this was ridiculous. "You mean you would cut the water off? I don't believe it."

"Ask Manuel."

Ask Manuel! Spoken as confidently as that, it must be true. Stunned, appalled, Claire could only stare straight ahead of her. June, her baby in her arms, gazed sweetly back. She found her tongue. "Señor Pascual," she exclaimed angrily, "you are a very wicked man."

"I look after my own."

The Spanish way! It had not taken her long to find out how thoroughly the Spaniard looked after his own. Claire's mind stampeded. She could not shrink from this appalling situation. She could not, as perhaps Ricardo was doing, put her head in the sand. Was Ricardo, then, prepared to see Manuel ruined? What was more to the point was: Am I prepared to see my mother's husband ruined? And for what? If she was to believe Rosita's father, for a man who might really be attracted by her good health, and inevitably, she knew herself, by her likeness to her mother whom Ricardo already loved.

TWELVE

The past came creeping back and laid itself before
Claire. Fate, with its diabolical timing, had given
her the prize part: to play Nemesis, an instrument
of revenge. It had given her an opportunity to ruin
her mother's family. Aunt Marcia might say:
"That's squaring the account." Marcia's God was
retributive. I can have Ricardo's love, Claire
thought, shaken, and at the same time make June
pay for all those motherless years.

She said: "What does my mother's going have to
do with you, Señor Pascual?"

"I didn't send her away."

And yet she had gone that afternoon Pascual
came to call. Had she really gone because of
Manuel's womanizing? Pascual had shed a new
light on the situation. It could well have been
because she was unable to face up to Manuel's
bullying of Ricardo. And that could explain the

fact that Manuel made no attempt to bring her back, because, since Ricardo had not capitulated, she would be coming back to the same situation. Can I make this promise to Pascual, then find a way to break it? It is being made to a bad man for the wrong reasons. But it has to be made. I have to see June, she thought feverishly.

She said in a hollow voice she scarcely recognized: "I promise. Now will you promise to let Manuel have the water?"

"Of course. You will go to your mother now. You are a good daughter," Pascual was saying. "A pencil and paper, then. You will not remember this address. The house is in the medina in Tangier."

"The *what*? Where?" she cried in dismay, already feeling tricked. Tangier was in Africa!

"The medina is the old, walled part of the city of Tangier which encloses the bazaar. You can get a taxi from the port, and then for a few *dirhams* any Arab boy will lead you into the medina. There you can ask for your mother's address."

"This is the native quarter?" Claire asked incredulously. "What would my mother be doing there?"

"It is a very private place to live. If you are rich you can live in the center of the town. The friends of your mother choose to live there," Pascual explained, "no doubt in a very fine house, for they can have guards on the entrances so they are safe from thieves, which is not so in the suburbs. The medina has some very fine houses. Have you a pencil?"

How did he know about these friends of June's? And then she remembered that Teresa had said the families grew close during the time Rosita was dangerously ill. With a heavy heart Claire wrote down the address. "How do I get to Tangier?"

"You will go by bus to Algeciras, then on the ferry. Or it is faster on the hydrofoil, but more expensive," Pascual said. "Or you could write," he added helpfully. "Or why not send a telegram?"

She already knew she was not going to do that. June's reasons for going had to be respected. Claire had no right to call her back before her problems were resolved, if indeed she was coming back at all. In a daze of misery and fright, she put the receiver down. She had never been truly in love before, and she did not know how she was going to relinquish this magic that had taken her in its grip. Do I owe my mother this? she asked herself bitterly as she went back up the stairs. Do I owe her my happiness and perhaps my future, when she has already, in a manner of speaking, taken my past? But it's her or me, if I can't find a way around this idiotic promise I've made.

She lay awake, staring out into the moonlight, listening to the distant murmur of the sea. Somewhere an owl hooted and once a great gust of wind sent the palm leaves slapping gently against the walls. She was still awake, hours later, when Manuel came home. She did not look at her watch because she did not want to know the time. Maybe he does only talk to men in bars. Maybe I misjudge him. It is all so different here. Tomorrow, whatever it costs, I will go. I cannot cope with those very naughty boys. Why cannot Manuel make them see sense? Marcia would say they need some good, old-fashioned, English discipline. Perhaps Juan really is ill and needs a doctor. I wonder if I can go to Tangier and back in a day? If Pascual has tricked me, then I must be able to get back.

* * * *

In the morning Claire found it surprisingly easy to leave. Manuel did not protest, and nor did he offer to drive her. Instead, he produced the keys of June's little Fiat and to Claire's astonishment, said gravely: "Keep it until Juanita returns." Manuel was not sleeping until midday today. Everything had changed at the villa, and not by any means for the better. Knowing he held her by the lifeline of the car, he seemed almost glad to see her go, and she was glad to be off before Ricardo put in an appearance. This morning, too, Oliva the maid's black eyes were hostile and already she could hear her in the kitchen shrilly regaling Tomasa with the disturbances of the day before. Juan was better and the two boys were playing a card game in his room. He was not allowed to get up yet.

"I will telephone the hotel and tell them you are coming," Manuel said, kissing her on both cheeks, holding her a little too tightly, a little too long, against his massive chest. His sexuality still bothered her, embarrassed her. She tried to tell herself it was as essential a part of him as the hair on his head but her thoughts kept returning to the night when he had come alone to the *finca* and thrown Ricardo and herself out. "Good-bye, little Claire," he said, lingering on the words. "We will see you back again soon."

At the last moment she remembered the tourist bureau leaflet she had tossed into the wastepaper basket and went back to retrieve it. She might find

some information here regarding Tangier, and if
not, at least it would show the address of the
bureau and she would be able to find the same
place again.

She found the tourist bureau easily enough.
Yes, said the clerk, it was possible to go to Tangier
in a day. She asked him what time she would have
to leave in order to return the same day if she
needed to.

"You are going alone?" She nodded. "We do a
very nice excursion. The coach would pick you up
at your hotel at five o'clock in the morning, you
would be shown Tangier, taken to the medina for
shopping, then returned to the hydrofoil or the
ferry, whichever you wish, in the evening. It
would not be advisable to make this journey alone
without a guide," the man said. "In a party you
will be looked after, and you will go to the places
you would like to see."

The apprehension peeled away. This, of
course, was the answer. "Would our guide be a
local man?"

"Yes. He would be an Arab." An Arab in a
responsible position would surely find her a
responsible guide to take her to the address
Pascual had given her. "I'll go on that excursion,"
she said.

She filled in the name of her hotel, and bought
her ticket. "The coach will pick you up at five
o'clock in the morning, you understand. You will
ask at your hotel for a call."

"Yes. I understand. By the way, I'm changing
my hotel. I'll call you and give you the name."

She tucked her ticket into her handbag and
went out into the street, well pleased. She drove

through the town looking at hotel fronts then eventually stopped at a small one in a leafy road on the waterfront side of the town. When she had checked in she drove back to the original one and cancelled the booking. No doubt Manuel would find her, if he wanted to, because of the car, but at least she could make it a little more difficult for him.

Walking around the town, she bought a flat basket that would serve as a shoulder bag and also carry a jacket and an extra pair of shoes. In the event that she should find June and be invited to stay the night, she could also have a change of underwear without it looking obvious that she had come expecting to stay. She threw the basket on the back seat of the car and climbed in.

It was a lonely day, but interesting. Claire wandered where the roads took her, going far up into the hills, walking among the wild flowers, pausing to explore the dazzling little white-painted hilltop villages, chatting to the occasional Spaniard who spoke English. An elderly man took her into his house and up to the roof to admire the view down mile after mile of leafy valley in its early summer green, the stream still running with the snow waters from the mountains, the grapes laddering the hillsides, in young leaf. "In September it will be all brown as the soil," he said, indicating the already relentless sun. A woman crocheting a fine shawl in her doorway invited Claire to a bedroom upstairs to view the stock she was preparing for the summer tourists. Claire bought a gossamer thin wrap and went on her way feeling heartened. She had lunch at the one restaurant the village boasted, run by an

Englishman with a French wife. "No," he said in answer to her astonished query, "we do not cater for the villagers. People know of us in Malaga and they come up in the evening for the drive and for my wife's cooking." Claire lingered on their vine-hung verandah during the excessive heat of the day while the village slept and was given the bonus of a cup of English tea.

It was seven o'clock when she returned to the hotel. The boy at the desk who handed her the key looked at her oddly. "You have had a nice day, Señorita?"

"Very nice, thank you." She went up in the elevator. She thrust her key in the lock then realized with surprise that the door was ajar. She pushed it open.

He was standing by the window, his face dark against the light. He did not speak, and neither did she at first. She threw her handbag and the basket on to the bed and put both hands over her face as though that would hide her from him. "Oh Ricardo!" He came towards her on silent feet and was gently undoing her fingers.

"You can't get away," he said with infinite tenderness.

"I must." It was more of a call for help than a statement of fact.

"But you cannot, and nor can I." He put both arms around her, kissing her lingeringly.

But she must not allow him to come after her. There was the promise to Pascual.

She pulled away saying the first thing that came into her head: "Ricardo, it's just because of my mother. You love my mother and I look like her. You want what Manuel has."

"It's not as simple as that." Ricardo held her hands, smiling down at her. "Of course I think Manuel is lucky."

"His marriage to my mother is a disaster."

"A disaster?" The dark brows shot up. "But of course it is a great success."

"Then why has she run away?"

"Because she was disturbed. A passing thing. Let us not talk of them. Claire, I love you."

The shadow of Rosita fell between them and with a nervous movement she withdrew. "You've only known me a few days. How did you find me?" she asked, feeling spied upon, hemmed in. On Friday Manuel had found her.

"It is easy enough if one knows a town."

"No, it's not that easy. This is quite a big town."

He chuckled. "Come. You will want to change for dinner."

"Ricardo, I cannot go out to dinner with you. I cannot."

"But of course you can." His blue eyes twinkled. "Now you must change. We seem to have been through this before, but you can be sure my mother will not come this time, to interfere. And you do not have a balcony in this room, so I will wait in the hall. How long will you be?"

"Ricardo, I can't go with you." And then she blurted it out, the truth that they had somehow managed to avoid. "You have to mar—You are tied up with—"

"Rosita? Claire, darling, I have many problems and Rosita is one of them."

Oh no! The situation could not be simplified like that! What did he mean? And then she looked at him with suddenly stricken eyes. Did Ricardo not know about the threat of withdrawal of the water? Perhaps not. Perhaps Pascual was relying on family pressure to move him, for common sense told her it would not be easy to live with a son-in-law in the tightly enclosed Spanish way if he had been forced to marry one's daughter in order to save his family from financial ruin. On the other hand, if Ricardo could be persuaded by Manuel that this marriage was right and proper, then that would perhaps be another matter.

Turning away, feeling tearful and vulnerable and angry, she repeated her refusal. "I cannot go out with you tonight."

"You're afraid of being seen?" With light fingertips on her shoulders, Ricardo drew her around to face him.

"Yes. I don't want to make trouble."

"Then I'll take you somewhere where we will certainly not be seen. Do you like fish?"

"Yes. Very much." She said it before she could stop herself, then bit her lips. She was frightened, now, of the effect Ricardo had on her. Was this what had happened to June all those years ago, with Manuel?

"Then get into an old pair of jeans," Ricardo said, "if you have them, and I'll take you to a fishermen's café down on the waterfront. I assure you," he said, laughing, "you will not meet any of my family there."

The temptation was more than she could bear. She fought and lost. "Just once," she said, holding his hand to her cheek, loving him in spite of Pascual and his crippled daughter, in spite of her promise, and Manuel's financial troubles.

He made a move towards the door. "I'll leave you to change."

Claire saw it at first as an escapade, and then as they dashed through the streets of Malaga a new feeling came over her, of having embarked on something that was outside her control. She tried to exorcise Manuel, Rosita and Pascual from her mind and give herself up to the dangerous moment, but it did not work. There was too much at stake. Ricardo parked the car beneath some tall trees on a small clearing on the outskirts of the town and they picked their way over the rough ground that ran down towards the shore. Moonlight showed up low square boxes of houses like sheds, each with one window and an open doorway in which stood a kitchen chair, the meagre comfort of the old and tired. Ancient-looking, often toothless, black-clad fisherwives, their skins as dry as autumn Spanish hills, glanced up curiously from their knitting or broke off their strident chatter to stare. Looking at them, Claire was intrigued, and at the same time a little shocked at her own comparative affluence.

They followed the dusty earth track towards the shore where the smell of sea dregs was heady in its intensity and a small fire in a hedge sent off a pungent scent from burning scales and tails. The restaurant was on the edge of the water. Tables were set among the pebbles and stones on a scruffy beach and discarded shells lay all over used tables. She turned to Ricardo. He was laughing. "You didn't want to be seen."

"Oh Ricardo!" She laughed with him. "Is this the sort of lesson you give to girls who try to make the rules?"

"Not at all," he said, suddenly solemn. "I thought you would like it."

Impulsively, she stood on tiptoes and kissed his cheek. "And so I do." A squat, dark woman with the biggest hips Claire had ever seen came over to their table. With one hand she swept away a bowl of empty shells, spilling some of them among the pebbles at their feet, then indicated that they might like to sit down. A middle-aged man with a collarless white shirt, picking his teeth at the table next door, nodded in friendly fashion. "Look," she said delightedly, "there's a fire at the end of the beach. What are those little silver fish stretched out on strips of wet wood?"

"Sardines. Try them. And some local wine? And shellfish?"

"Oh yes." They watched the waitress taking their sardines from the open fire, all black and silver and scented from the wood. A wild-looking fisherman in a black cap at the next table who had laughing eyes and an evil moustache raised his glass of wine to her.

"*Salud, Señorita.*"

"Cheers," she said, and gaily raised hers.

Claire was a little drunk, with the fear and the excitement and the wine. With her love for Ricardo, too. He had removed his neat shirt in the car and taken an old cotton pullover from the trunk. He looked very much at home with the fishermen, exchanging greetings and lively comments, roaring with laughter at their jokes, translating them to Claire. Impetuously, she reached across the table and touched his wrists. "Ricardo, what will happen if you don't marry Rosita?"

He said gravely: "It will be uncomfortable, living in the town. But I am not likely to be staying there much longer. You know that. If my hospital plans are accepted, then I shall be working in Malaga. And if they are not, I shall have to look in Malaga or Granada for work."

She scarcely heard him after the first sentence. Sick with despair, she thought: That's it. He doesn't know. It's between the families, this threat. Or rather, between Manuel and Pascual.

THIRTEEN

Claire woke with a start. The telephone at her bedside was buzzing monotonously. Disorientated, confused, she fumbled with the receiver, thinking that she had only just drifted into sleep. She heard a man say something in Spanish and opening her eyes realized that she was in a hotel in Malaga, Spain, and it was time to get up to catch a bus that would take her to the mother she did not remember. Stunned by the crude awakening, overwhelmed by a sense of total unreality, she flopped back on to the pillows.

What if Pascual was sending her off on a wild goose chase? Spain, two weeks ago, had been foreign enough. But Africa, the dark continent! And on a bus? I'm mad, she thought, gathering her senses. This isn't possible. Africa is a world away, and besides, I cannot face it on my own. Why hadn't she told Ricardo? They could have

gone together if Ricardo had thought it sensible.
Panic. Her stomach started to roll and then she
had to get up quickly and go to the bathroom to be
sick.

There was no time to lie back in bed to recover.
Shakily, she began to look for something to wear.
At four-thirty the morning was cool. The room
was light but the sky outside was pale, a little
bleak. Spanish girls, she had noticed, did not wear
jeans very much. Teresa's clothes were not
elegant but they were pretty. Claire did not have
the sort of dress Teresa would wear. She
compromised with a soft peasant blouse and
gathered skirt. She was half-dressed when a tap
came at the door. Flinging on her robe, she opened
it. A servant stood there with a tray. The pungent
scent of coffee made her stomach retch. She
signed to the man to take the tray away and shut
the door quickly. I'll be all right when I'm calmer,
she said to herself. It was a shock, that telephone
ringing when I was too deeply asleep. And
apprehension. Stomach nerves. Wasn't this what
had happened to Juan?

Or had he caught some bug and handed it on to
her? Heavens! How could she know at a quarter to
five in the morning? She sat down on the bed,
considering the situation. Am I ill? Am I really ill,
in which case I cannot go to North Africa on a bus
and boat, alone. North Africa! It was frightening
enough to contemplate when in the best of health
for she had to face up to the fact that Pascual could
conceivably be lying to her. Why should he know
June's whereabouts? Her exact address? What
sort of person was he? He was certainly corrupt.
Was he also evil? It occurred to her for the first

time that he could be sending her to some dark alley from which she might never return.

No, that's ridiculous, she told herself firmly. I can check. I'll find someone who speaks English. I'll make inquiries somehow. I wouldn't, as Pascual suggested, give some Arab boy a few coins and follow him blindly down snaking, high-walled alleys. Beside, there will be English tourists on the bus. I'll get some help from someone.

The telephone rang again and she jumped. The bus must have arrived. There was no time to think, no time to worry any more. She had to go. She would be all right. Her stomach would settle down. Sanity would come with daylight. She whipped the new basket out of the wardrobe and began to throw in makeup, a hairbrush, a change of underwear and shoes, a toothbrush, some tissues. She upended her handbag, shook the contents into the basket. She ran out of the door, then latently went back to lock it behind her. Over to the elevator, pressing the button, then back again for her ticket, lying uselessly on the dressing table. Her head was spinning. The bell was ringing again. She threw a panicky look at the telephone, locked the door and took the stairs three at a time.

The bus driver was impatient, threatening to go without her. It was too early in the morning for kindness. Too hurried for charm. Claire stumbled up the steps, the door silently imprisoned her and the bus moved off. There was a further moment of uneasiness mounting rapidly to anxiety as she realized the people on board were foreigners. Even the pair who looked faintly English began to talk in German. They called at another hotel, and another. Fair-haired people came aboard. She brightened, then they spoke and her heart sank, for they too were German. Another call and the coach was full. Any frail hopes Claire retained were now dashed.

They swept down the long main highway past tall blocks of apartments, luxury hotels, and pretty new bungalows with tall palm trees and oleander in their gardens, the stone walls cloaked in cascades of purple, red and orange bougainvillaea. Through Torremolinos, Fuengirola, Marbella, Estepona; grey rocky mountains to the right of them, the silver sea to the left; dashing through time, through nineteen years at a hundred kilometers an hour; the lion-shaped rock of Gibraltar growing larger and larger. And then there was Africa, a shading of gray hills in the morning sky. Africa; Arabs in long gowns and bare feet, a labyrinthine city of concrete and barred doors, dust and long knives in the night. An address that perhaps she had been a fool to accept. Stop worrying. Keep calm. You cannot be sick on a bus. You cannot be sick on a bus. Was that a town out in front? Were they actually approaching Algeciras? You don't have to go into the medina. You can throw this address away and come back to Malaga this evening. Come back, without even trying to find June? How can you do that? You don't feel ill. It's imagination. Psychosomatic. Nerves.

They ran in through the dusty, leafy suburbs with their white-painted houses; around the waterfront past tall blocks of flats. At the port they left the bus and were hustled through a building, across an acre of concrete and into the waiting hydrofoil. Claire found the bathroom. There was a twisting in her stomach now that she knew had nothing at all to do with apprehension. Nothing to do with nerves. It was time to stop pretending. Last night, in that intriguing waterfront café, in the excitement of Ricardo's arrival, with the guilt and the fear in her, memory, common sense, self-preservation, all had gone by the board. The last time she ate shellfish, and that was years ago for she had not dared do it since, she had been very ill indeed. She felt the craft move away from the wharf, felt it rise on its strange skis, knew they were headed out into the straits of Gibraltar and there was no going back. Perhaps, she thought giddily, if I am ill now, while we are at sea, I will be all right by the time we arrive. In the tiny mirror over the washbasin her face was white as a sheet.

A black-haired, black-eyed attendant watched her apprehensively as she looked for a seat in the lounge. Patently concerned, he came down the gangway in his long striped djellaba and his little red fez to hand her a paper bag.

She sat very still watching the sparkling showers of spray against the windows, watching Africa grow bigger and browner and more real. She tried not to think about anything. What was to be would be. At last the engines cut and they slid in to a wharf where dark-skinned, black-eyed, barefooted men in baggy white trousers rolled up to the knees, ran around like rabbits making the vessel fast. Oh, the pain in her stomach! She rushed back to be sick again but before she reached the door the feeling went.

Tall, brown-faced men in painted yellow sandals. Bare-footed, curly-haired, black-eyed, begging boys. Men in long striped gowns hanging loosely over European clothes. Men with cotton hoods to shield them from the sun. "*Dirhans*, lady?" "English pounds?" They knew the begging words in every language. Claire was glad to get on the bus. She had a feeling of nearing the end of her tether and she did not know what to do. The bus took off. There was a wonderful curve of beach, white lacy waves, tall, graceful palms and a lot of scruffy waterfront cafés with dirty windows, their paintless tables scattered higgledy-piggledy on the pavements. The blazing, burning sun. Pink hibiscus and a jutting promontory thickly encrusted with a coat of houses and apartments so brilliantly white they blinded in the sun.

The bus turned its back on the town. Their guide, having established that there were four nationalities aboard, attended last to the lone Englishwoman. "There is the medina, on your right, behind." Claire heard it as they sped up a hill covered in scrub, too late to look back, and then they were looking down on a vast and beautiful beach with a coastal plain and low foothills behind. She felt as though she was being borne irreversibly into the unknown.

The pain was creeping through her again, twisting her entrails. Claire stared obsessively at what they had been brought to see, filling her mind with the view in order to try to exclude the sickness and pain. Tiny haystacks, small camels lying in long dry grass; caramel-colored cattle with cream horns, grazing. If she kept her mind on the scenery the pain would give up and go away. What you ignore cannot survive.

Of course the problem was brought on by excitement. The kind of nerves that had made Juan ill. Of course. Of course. Nothing to do with shellfish. Look at the eucalyptus trees bordering the flat white road. At the square white houses bunched together on a swathe of green like a top-knot on a conical hill. Look at the donkeys grazing, and you won't feel the pain. Heavens, it was only ten-thirty in the morning, and so terribly hot. Hot, and yet icily cold. There was cactus spread across the hillside, a round tent covered with Arabic. Maize. Beds of dwarf tomato plants bearing toy fruit. A donkey carrying water bottles. No, it was not possible to be ill on a bus, besides you do not feel ill, only a bit giddy and you will be better soon if you concentrate on other things. Look at that dirty, dark man wearing a wool hat with a pom-pom.

She had long ago given up trying to follow the guide's patter. She no longer knew when the Spanish ended and the English began for he rattled from one language to the next in the same tone. Green and gold melons piled on a balcony rail; square houses with frail looking bamboo walls; wise brown sheep with spatulate tails. Then the coach was heading back towards the town and there, perched like a pinhead on a donkey's load, was a bride swathed in white and silver, black eyes gazing tranquilly beneath a huge white hat and over an enveloping veil. Claire's excitement subjugated the pain and then, miraculously, it went.

She heard the word "medina" emerge from a spate of German. They drove slowly down a narrow street crowded by dirty white buildings, dirty gray buildings where dogs and children ran ahead in the dust. There was a turbanned gentleman sitting cross-legged on the pavement playing a pipe. Snakes rose from a sack before him. The bus paused and everyone craned their necks. Then they were climbing out. Claire mingled with the crowd walking slowly up a roughly paved slope to an enormous stone gateway, keeping in the shade of the high walls, praying that she would not have another attack. Now she knew she had to make an effort to locate this address. If June was here, then she had to find her. It was not likely that she could feel so ill and then, miraculously, recover. When they entered the medina she would speak to the guide. Perhaps he would know someone who could find out for her if June was here. A touch on the hand and she turned to see an urchin in a ragged, filthy white gown split to the waist. He was offering her something from his half-open hand. "Missy buy lucky stones." She smiled at him and shook her head.

At the gate the guide counted his charges. A peddlar in a white singlet and jeans crept around a shadowed stone column holding a silver watch in his hand. "You buy watch? Very good price," he whispered, one dark eye on the guide. The guide saw and hurled abuse at him. The man scuttled off. "Don't buy from these people in the street," the guide said. "I take you to big shop for Europeans. Everything the right price. Is what you want. Is where Europeans in Tangier do shopping."

Claire felt in her basket for the wallet containing the address Pascual had given her. Obediently, the crowd turned to follow the guide. She felt another touch on her arm. Without turning her head, she shook the hand off, then felt the fingers grip and hold. She swung around nervously. "Nice silver watch, Missy?"

"Ricardo!" She closed her eyes, then opened them again and miraculously, he was still there. It was like an act of God. Something that was meant to be. Ricardo of the sapphire eyes, the jutting cheekbones, the shining black hair. She forgot she had exchanged her right to love him for her mother's address. She forgot she was ill. She grasped his hand convulsively, holding it between her own. "How did you get here? How did you know?"

The guide was standing tall, looking over the heads of the crowd. The rest of the party had gone on. "Better keep up," Ricardo advised, taking Claire's arm and giving her a gentle little push. "The joke's on me," he explained wryly. "I found out where you were going. I intended to be at your hotel just before the coach. I was going to whisk you away in my car, but the car wouldn't start. I broke all traffic regulations, but still missed the hydrofoil by inches."

"But how did you know?" They were hurrying after the party, through narrow streets high-walled on either side. A donkey and its white-robed owner wandered past and then a woman driving three caramel-colored goats. An open-fronted shop spilled its wares on to the pavement. The guide drove his flock on, determined they should not stop to buy at any but the approved store.

"If you want to hide your movements, dear Claire," said Ricardo, eyes dancing, "don't throw tourist pamphlets round. I saw it go into the wastepaper basket.

"I retrieved it."

"Yes, but not before I'd seen it. I knew where it came from. I checked with the office. They told me you had booked on a Tangier excursion and gave me the name of your hotel." So that was how he had found her yesterday! "I have many friends in Malaga. Why didn't you ask me to take you? I could have given you a much more exciting day, quite exclusive," Ricardo added jauntily, "and absolutely free. Besides, the best way to see a place is with local people and we have friends in Tangier."

June's friends? In such a close-knit family would they not be likely to know each other's friends? Maybe she had misjudged Pascual. Claire felt absurdly happy. "You didn't say you would come."

"You didn't say you were going." They laughed together. The party crowded after the guide through dusty, twisting, high-walled gray streets. The sun flared like a torch across the upper western walls. The shadows were razor-sharp.

"Lucky stones, very cheap." The whispering voice crept upon Claire's ear. The guide was shooing itinerant peddlars away. "Come," he called again, a messiah-life figure in his long robe with that imperious arm held high. "Don't buy from these boys," he shouted. "They are thieves."

"He's taking us to a big store that sells the sort of thing tourists buy," Claire explained.

"I know the one. What do you want? What can I buy you, darling?"

"You mustn't buy me anything. I, on the other hand, may buy myself a caftan." They had turned another corner and there in front of them was a tall building with barred windows. Outside, a conglomeration of earthenware pots, leather goods and wrought-iron. Ricardo released her arm. She moved forward, listening, waiting for the English version as the guide gave instructions as to what they should do. There was an hour to spare, he said, and they could spend it in this store where there was everything they were likely to want to buy. Suddenly she saw a flash of anger cross the guide's face. He ran around the outside of the party towards Claire, then stopped short. Turning, she saw that a small Arab boy had detained Ricardo, and Ricardo was looking interestedly at a handful of rings. "I thought the boy was bothering you," the guide said to Claire, ushering her safely away, "but it is the gentleman. He is not of the party. You must not buy from the street," he advised her again. "You do not get the value. Now, you will go here, please." He ushered her firmly towards the doorway of the store and she went, knowing Ricardo would follow.

It was an Aladdin's cave of a place. There were three floors built around a balconied court. Claire stood in the doorway, marveling. Blankets bright as an African sky, huge leather cushions decorated with painted camels and palm trees; silver and stones. Great gaudy rock jewels from the desert in glass cases, rubies, amethysts, turquoises. Exciting, flamboyant, beautiful things to tempt you on the day, then let you down when you took them home. Fake diamonds and fake silver already turned dull in the heat and the dust that was everywhere. There were gaudy painted slippers with pointed toes; leather stools and brass tables. She was still standing fascinated when Ricardo caught her up. "I bought you a little present," he said.

"Oh Ricardo," she protested, "you shouldn't buy from the street boys. The guide says it's highly priced rubbish."

"When on vacation one must do what one wants to do. Of course you must shop here because our friend gets a commission, but I am not with the party so I may waste my money with impunity." He lifted her hand and slipped a ring on the third finger. For a moment she was too surprised to speak. "Move your hand," he said. "See, it changes from pale to dark and back to pale again." The stone was pinkish in one light, ruby red when she turned it, and mauve in another. It appeared to be set in white gold, but of course it would be silver for all the rings in the glass boxes on the counter before her were set in silver, and silver, or imitation silver, was everywhere.

Ricardo said softly: "It will bring you your dearest wish." He looked gravely into her eyes, then kissed her.

She did not want to take the ring. She said, her voice high and trembling, a little out of control:

"Lucky stone, as the boy said. It's an Alexandrite, isn't it?"

Ricardo's face went still. Then: "How did you know?" he asked.

"I didn't know, at first. I've just realized. It's such an unusual color. A friend of mine had one. They're all synthetic, aren't they, except the fabulously expensive and rare ones that come out of Russia."

He said dryly: "You're well informed." She turned away, flushing, realizing she had been unforgivably tactless in saying the stone was synthetic, for Ricardo was hurt. She should have taken it as the lovely gesture it was, like having the Christmas tree fairy's halo put around one's wrist. Ricardo held up a tiny silver charm. "And this is for me," he dropped it carelessly into his wallet. "I shall wish on that."

As suddenly as it had gone, the pain came again. Claire back-tracked again. It's nerves, just like Juan. She could not, would not be ill now. Only nerves, and that I can control. Why, otherwise, should I feel fine until something goes a little bit wrong?

"Come on upstairs," suggested Ricardo, taking her arm, "and look at these caftans. I'll buy you one to go with your gold shoes." He looked at her concernedly. "What's the matter?"

She tried to laugh about it. "I've actually been ill all morning. And I've been having some pains. But suddenly the pain went and I thought—" She had not thought at all. Ricardo had come in like a magic wand.

"Juan was ill," Ricardo reminded her. "Perhaps he had a bug. Perhaps you've caught it." He took her hands, looking concernedly into her face. "You're very pale. I should have noticed."

It was starting all over again, and now Claire knew she could not ignore it. Her forehead was suddenly on fire and the rest of her body had once again gone cold. Icy cold this time and the demon pain was an agony. She gave a little cry, felt her head go light as though it was made of cotton wool, felt her knees buckle and saw the floor coming up to meet her in a black void.

Dark heads, dark, curious faces peering into hers. The brush of human beings round her, sharp orders and a scatter of feet. Then pain came again, and again. Claire went into a world of blackness; again returned. She was aware of being carried; of noisy excitement; of shouting; of walls closing in on her and the clatter of feet on stones; of a feeling of panic because she was unable to control her destiny; because she did not know whose arms held her. Ricardo's concerned face. Blessed relief. "I'm all right now," she whispered. "I can stand." And then the excruciating pain took her and twisted her into circles of agony beyond bearing.

When she came around again they were on a cool, dark stairway. Ricardo said: "We're nearly there." She could see pillars, shadows, then bright sunlight. All round were murmurs of consternation and the soft swish of feet on tiles. They entered a shuttered room and Ricardo lowered her gently on to a bed. There was a tall woman with very black hair parted severely down the center and aquiline features. She said: "Lie very still. It is best. Someone is coming with a bowl of water. I will bathe your face. The doctor will be here soon,

I am sure. He lives very near, in the medina, and one of the servants has gone for him."

Claire was only vaguely aware of the doctor, of swallowing some foul tasting mixture and then going off into a state of further unconsciousness that must have turned to dreamless sleep for when she awakened she was calm. Calm, but drained. The room was dark but she could make out the form of someone sitting on her bed. "Ricardo?" she whispered.

The person moved and Claire saw it was a woman. She rose, crossed the room to open a window, then pushed the shutters back a few inches so that light filtered in. She was tall, with soft blonde hair, a full, oval face and gray eyes. Her broad forehead was unlined and she had a broken hairline like Claire's own, with short tendrils breaking away.

"What a way to meet," said Claire, her voice breaking.

June bent down and kissed her on the cheek. "I'm sorry," she said, sending a snowball of questions and confusions into Claire's mind.

"I'm sorry too," Claire said and burst into tears.

FOURTEEN

Claire could not stop crying. It was just that she was weak, she whispered, frantically mopping up the tears as they poured down her cheeks. The tubby little doctor who had been called back stood at her bedside shaking his head, clicking his tongue and frowning. June had disappeared and the tall dark woman whom the doctor addressed as Señor Cervera was evidently explaining in Arabic what the upset was about. "The doctor says you are to be kept very quiet. He is going to give you a strong sedative."

"I'm sorry. I can't help it." The tears poured out in a renewed flood.

"Of course," the woman said kindly. "We all understand."

"Where is my mother?"

"She had to go out." But there was a faint

evasiveness about the answer and Claire felt certain it was not the truth.

"Is Ricardo here?"

The woman looked uncomfortable, met the doctor's eyes, then said: "I will see if he has gone." The doctor put his bag on the bed and proceeded to search in it. Briskly, he produced a tiny glass and poured out a measure of some white liquid. Claire felt for the ring but it was not there. Momentarily, there was shock, a sense of enormous loss, a ridiculous feeling of desolation out of all proportion to the problem. It was, after all, only a cheap bazaar bauble, a synthetic stone set in some sort of base metal. But the shock of its disappearance closed her throat and she could not swallow. The doctor stood by her bed, tut-tutting while a new flood of tears engulfed her. Perhaps Ricardo himself had removed the ring so that June would not think her new daughter was given to wearing trashy jewelry. A servant in bunched white robes crossed the room, went through a door into a tiled bathroom and returned with a bowl of water and a towel. The dark woman said from somewhere behind her: "Just a little wash, I think, my dear, and then we will leave you to rest." She came around the head of the bed and smiled kindly down on the patient.

"Where is my mother?"

"It's better if you talk to her when you are a little better. This meeting has been a shock to you both."

Of course. But she had a feeling of having chased June away. The tears renewed themselves again. The woman picked up Claire's hand, held it gently between her own, looked down on the girl with compassion. "It's better to think of nothing. Just sleep and let the medicine do its work. I have another nightdress for you. It's mine. I'm sure it's not at all to your taste," she smiled, "but it's clean and cool."

"You're very kind. Who are you?"

"I am Miranda Cervera."

And Cervera was the name Pascual had given her.

The servant had turned back the hot sheet and was bathing Claire with a cool cloth and gentle hands. Her enormous black eyes were compassionate too, as though she knew there was more than sickness in the room. "I am glad you have come," said Señora Cervera. "Very glad."

"Why did my mother run away?"

"You must talk to her about that," the señora replied, but there was no rejection in her voice.

"I want to know now. I would like to think about it quietly before seeing her. I don't feel strong enough for—surprises." She was afraid of the tears. "Is it because Manuel goes with other women? And has she left him for good? Please tell me, Señora, so that I'm prepared when I talk to her."

Her hostess laughed lightly. "Juanita would never leave Manuel for good. And I do not think any woman could ever come between them. Yes, if you are worried, then this is something you should know. It is another issue. It is not to do with their love. Believe me, my dear, when Juanita gave up her baby she did not do it for a flight of fancy. She got something very wonderful—very, very wonderful—in exchange."

Claire smiled. "I needed to know that." She felt the drift of a new calm and felt herself relax a little more against the pillows.

When she came back to consciousness again night had fallen. In the faint light from a tiny lamp at her bedside she could just see round the room. She pulled herself very carefully into a sitting position. Her head felt heavy, her mind fuddled. She climbed slowly and tentatively out of bed, crossed the room and stood in the bathroom doorway steadying herself against the door post. There was a nightlight here, too, and with the aid of its soft glow she could see an enormous bath sunk into the tiled floor; shining gold taps that caught the light; she had a vague impression of dark blue and white; of Arabic signs and mosaic; a lot of fluffy towels. Her feet moved over a big, soft mat. She turned one of the gold taps and splashed cool water on to her face. The air was cooler in here because the window was open.

Back in the bedroom she lifted a slim iron bar and pushed the wooden shutters outwards. Thick vine encircled the window. Above, the sky was velvet black with stars like ice diamonds and a stately minaret flood-lit with gold against the darkness. She filled her lungs with the fresh night air and felt it creep past her into the hot room. Directly below, a light went on, and a balcony leaped into view. Though the light was merely an overspill she could see potted palms and geraniums. Some exotic trailing plants hung over the stone balustrade. There was the shadowy shape of a big chair and a small table. Two figures appeared, a man and a woman. Their voices floated upwards. Presently some bells began to ring, echoing over the town. An eerie, eastern cry, a wailing, rose from the minaret as the faithful were called to prayer.

From below came a sharp exclamation. Claire glanced down. The man had turned. She could now see his profile clearly in the light from the inner room. It was Ricardo. His head was high, arrogantly so. The woman turned towards him and now the light fell on her face. June, angry too. Claire felt a little quiver of fear go through her. She could not hear the soft words that passed between them. Then June held her hands beseechingly towards Ricardo, and Ricardo swung away. The distant wailing of the prayer rose and fell, cloaking the city with the sound, filtering down among the tall buildings, echoing and creeping among the alleys, swirling up. Ricardo turned slowly. There was an air about him as of a man driven. June was talking again, passionately. Ricardo shook his head, and shook it again and again. The wailing swirled away, faded. Claire caught a phrase. ". . . too soft with you." Ricardo flashed back angrily but his words were lost as the wailing rose again.

The night air was suddenly cold, and Claire was trembling. The trembling turned to something stronger that she could not control. Frightened, she made her way on wobbly legs back to bed and pulled the blankets up around her. The shivering continued. . . . *too soft with you . . . too soft with you . . . too soft*. What did June mean? Manuel loved his brothers. That she already knew. He loved his whole family. And her hostess had said there was nothing wrong between Manuel and June, that they loved each other. Nothing wrong, except that there was an issue. . . .

She had guessed June left because she could not bear to see Manuel force Ricardo into this marriage with Rosita. But, did she have it the wrong way round? Not wanting to face the implications of the words she had heard, Claire drifted into an unhappy no-man's-land halfway between sleeping and waking. She dreamed she was out in the snow, pulling at a covering that would not move. After a while she was aware that someone stood by her bed. Señor Cervera said concernedly: "Are you all right? I thought I heard a cry. You've opened the shutters and the room is cold." She touched one of Claire's hands and immediately gave an exclamation of alarm.

Claire drifted back into that cold, strange, dreamlike place from which Miranda Cervera had taken her. . . . *too soft with you*. Then the bedclothes were stirring as someone pushed a hot water bottle into the bed. Warmth seeped through to her cold feet and the dream began to recede. Someone was throwing an extra cover over her. Claire came gradually more awake, but when she opened her eyes she was alone again. The nightlight still glowed. Automatically, she felt for the ring Ricardo had given her. This time its disappearance was unacceptable. She sat up and looked around feverishly for her basket. She found it leaning against the table by her bed. She lifted it and tipped the contents on to the bed cover. She went through her purse, shook out tissues and underclothes. The ring was not there. She fell back against the pillows, leaving the things where they lay. The basket lost balance and fell, rattling softly along the floor.

It was several days before Claire felt better, and stronger. "Where is Ricardo?" she asked when Miranda Cervera brought her lunch.

"He had to go back home. He left many messages for you, hoping you will soon be well, but he had to leave without saying good-bye because the doctor did not want you disturbed," Miranda Cervera lied, not meeting Claire's eyes as she busied herself adjusting the tray and shaking out a clean white napkin. "Of course you know men have to work," she added lightly. She sat down in a chair by the bed. "I'll stay with you while you have your meal."

"It's very kind of you, but I am not a bit hungry."

"No, of course. But it's very important that you eat, otherwise you will never be strong. I'm sorry the food is so bland but that's what the doctor ordered. You are over the poisoning now, and it is just a matter of getting strong again. So the sooner you start eating the better," her hostess said firmly.

"I ate some shellfish."

"Yes. Ricardo has confessed he took you to a place on the waterfront in Malaga that might not have been very clean. He was upset about it. But it was very wrong of him, you know. If he had not done it you would not have been ill."

"It was my fault. I've been ill before from eating shellfish. I forgot." Bewitched by Ricardo's presence, she had forgotten a good deal that should be remembered.

"So ill?"

"Perhaps not." The señora nodded her head with satisfaction, shifting the blame back to Ricardo where no doubt they had all decided it belonged. Obediently, Claire ate the milky pudding which was made from goats' milk and was not to her taste.

"There is the question of your mother," said Miranda Cervera. "The doctor has asked her to stay away during your illness. She doesn't want you to think that she doesn't care. She would have liked to nurse you, but the doctor forbade it." She smiled, a nice, kind, friendly smile. "It must be very disturbing to meet one's mother almost for the first time." And then, without waiting for a reply: "Would you like to dress and come downstairs? You might have mint tea later, in the drawing room. Your clothes have been laundered and are hanging in the wardrobe."

"That was very kind."

Her hostess waved her thanks away. "We're not short of servants in Tangier." She rose from her chair. "I'll leave you now. This is a rambling old house, full of twisting corridors. I'll come back for you if you like."

"I'm sure I'll find my way."

"Then cross the landing outside your door and come down one flight of stairs. The staircase is an enclosed unit. The drawing room is on the first floor, off a small passageway on the right. It's better that you find your own way, so you won't be hurried. If there's anything you want, please let me know."

When she had dressed, Claire opened the door and went out on to an open tiled area, a sort of cloister that ran around the center of the house with doors in the inner wall. There were pillars and a balustrade round the edge. In the court below there was a fountain, a table, some chairs, enormous urns holding big-leafed plants and cactus. Above, a glass dome let in the light to show up the beautiful mosaic of the floor. Two dark-skinned, barefooted Arab boys were standing side by side looking bored. Their ankle-length, collarless gowns, unbuttoned to the chest, hung loosely from their bony little shoulders. Oddly, although Claire's footsteps were slow and must have been almost silent, they had heard her, or else they sensed that someone was watching them for they both looked up, two pairs of black eyes in milk chocolate faces. One of them started visibly, then with an exuberant bound disappeared into the lower cloister. She did not hear his bare feet on the stairs but a moment later he came running towards her, a broad grin on his face. She smiled uncertainly while he searched in the folds of his djellaba. Taking out a small package, he thrust it into her hands.

"Thank you." Puzzled, she unfolded the tissue. The ring! Ricardo's ring! Overwhelmed with emotion, she could only stare down at it. It winked up at her, in the shaft of sunlight that crept over the edge of the balcony. "Thank you," she repeated. "Thank you very much." He nodded and skipped happily away. Claire swung around, opened the door of her room and went back inside. She sat down in the big chair turning the ring around and around in the light. It might be a cheap bauble, but it was incredibly beautiful. She slipped it on her finger. Now it looked like a ruby.

She flicked her finger and it was pale again, not like a ruby at all. Something slid out of the wrapping and fell to the floor. She leaned down and picked up a note.

Ricardo's writing was small but bold. *Darling. Wear it when your mother is not there to see. She would not approve. And remember, if you wish on it all your wishes will come true. I am sorry to have to go without saying good-bye. It was necessary.* There was no signature.

The stone flickered into a thousand different shades of pinks and bluish pinks and reds. Claire had never owned any jewelry. She was no judge of value. But the idea persisted that the ring did not look like bazaar junk. Where did these Arab boys get their wares? Was it possible this was a good ring that had been stolen? No, of course not, she told herself sensibly. She knew it was very difficult to tell the difference between a real stone and a synthetic one. Even jewelers sometimes had to make tests. Come to think of it, Ricardo would scarcely have trusted this servant boy with anything of value. But Ricardo had said: *If you wish on it* . . . She held the ring momentarily against her cheek and made her wish. Then she slipped it into her purse and tucked the purse carefully into the bottom of her basket. She was smiling now, her spirit high. Out on the upper cloister again, she glanced down into the well below. June and Miranda Cervera were looking up, smiling expectantly, June looking exactly like her daughter but for the years. She was wearing a pink cotton dress gathered at the waist and white shoes. Her hair was soft, falling below her ears.

Beside her elegant, black-haired hostess she looked very soft and gentle. Very English indeed for a woman who had spent the last nineteen years in a foreign land.

"Wait," June called. "I'll come and get you. We don't want you falling down the stairs."

All at once there was a clamp around Claire's heart. "I'll be all right," she said in a cool voice.

But June came running. Claire could hear the clatter of her shoes on the tiles. She arrived breathless and laughing, so warm and affectionately concerned that Claire felt herself softening. "It's quite ridiculous," she exclaimed, "that we should be so alike!" No wonder the barman had recognized Claire as a relative that first day she arrived in Spain!

"Yes, we are, aren't we?" June stood back and looked at her, then smoothed her hair back from her forehead and kissed her tenderly. "It's lovely to see you so much better, but oh dear, how pale you are. We must get you out into the air. The medina is too enclosed."

They went slowly, clinging together. It had never been like this with Aunt Marcia, Claire remembered with a pang. Aunt Marcia had loved Claire but perhaps she had not been motherly. June was intensely female. She seemed to exude a warm, protective, scented aura that wrapped itself around her daughter. "When you're stronger, perhaps tomorrow, we'll take you for a drive and show you what's outside the city," June said. "The views of the Atlas Mountains are superb. When you're strong enough to walk we can visit the Sultan's palace. It's sad that this disaster should have occurred before Ricardo had time to show you anything."

"Yes." So Ricardo had not told them Claire came alone! They went slowly and carefully down the shadowed stairs with June holding her daughter's arm. By the time they reached the drawing room Claire's knees were wobbling badly. Her mother sat her down swiftly in a chair. "Thanks. Heavens, I am weak!"

"You'll be all right soon. Food, rest and fresh air, that's what you need."

She was seated in an enormous and immensely glamorous room, or rather a series of rooms connected by decorative arches. There were Turkish rugs and animal skins on the floor, ornate mirrors on the walls, beautiful pictures, fat cushioned sofas. Claire said, laughing weakly: "It's a bit like the Arabian Nights. I feel disorientated. What a place to hold our first talk!" She glanced up and suddenly something outside her control took over. "I don't suppose I could talk when you left." Immediately after she had said it she could have bitten her tongue out, yet she knew, confusedly, that something like that had to be said. It was no use pretending she felt nothing for the lost years. There was too much awareness in her now of what she had missed. It was going to come out and perhaps it was better now than later. Better to clear the air and start afresh.

"No," said June, speaking carefully and looking rather hard at one of her fingernails. "No, you couldn't talk. So yes, it is the first time. Claire, let me say this quickly before—before—" Their eyes met and June seemed to see confirmation of what

she feared "—before you begin by punishing me,"
she finished quietly. "I may deserve punishment.
Or you may think I do, but I want to tell you my
side of the story first before you say too much."

FIFTEEN

Undoubtedly the interview would have gone far
better if Claire had been more herself. In her weak
state she could feel the weight of the motherless
years. *Everyone has a mother but me, Aunt Marcia.
Why haven't I?* Reclining on an overstuffed sofa in
that weirdly Eastern room, Claire was besieged
by a confusion of emotions. She lifted her eyes to
the molded plasterwork panels on the walls,
decorated like tapestry with pine cones and
vegetables; rich oriental traceries; a frieze with an
inscription in some Eastern lettering. "Why do
the Cerveras live in this—palace?"

June looked up. "Because they're rich.
Miranda's had several husbands, each one better
off than the last. She hasn't had good luck with
them, though. Perhaps as a result of her
experiences she's very wise and kind. I've known
her for many years. I met her when I first came to

Spain and she was a great comfort to me—about you, I mean. She taught me to accept, and to rise above my problems. Then she lost her Spanish husband and I hope I was able, in some measure, to help her. Manuel and I come often to Tangier to stay with her, and she and her present husband, an American of Spanish descent, come to us."

"It was very good of her to take me in."

"She would help my children, any time."

My children! The subject had to be broached. "I have to call you something," Claire said. "You won't expect me to call you Mother?" The reason behind the question was suspect and her mother would know.

"Could you call me Juanita?"

Something verging on childish rebelliousness rose up in Claire. The Spaniards had taken her English mother. Did they have to ram home their crime? "Why should you call yourself by a Spanish name?"

"I'm Spanish now," said June gently. "Do you want me to be a foreigner in my husband's country? To be called by a Spanish name is a part of the fitting in." She turned away sharply, looking out over the rooftops. "You may call me anything you like," she said quietly. "It's not important. Not by comparison with what's happening now." Turning back, with an impulsive movement she took Claire's hands. "We must talk. It's a little late, I know. I've been putting it off on the orders of the doctor because you were in no condition to be disturbed emotionally. But we're mother and daughter. We have to get this relationship set somehow. I know you're resentful of the fact that I've been asked to stay in the background so you could have what your father and his relations considered the right sort of upbringing." All at once June's eyes were brimming. "I've done this for you, and I want you to know. You don't understand. I can see it in your eyes. I, too, have always thought what I accepted was wrong, and perhaps I should have been firmer."

It was as though her mother's distress poured over Claire in waves and it was all she could do to stand calmly against it. But there were questions to be asked and answered before the way ahead could be cleared. She must not give way to emotion. "What made you write? Two letters only I received, but Ricardo said there were more."

June's eyes were still moist. "Not many more. Perhaps half a dozen. Those tentative little efforts I made to get in touch were a sort of disobedience. And then sending Ricardo to your school. It was wrong, I knew that. And it didn't work, so I suppose," she added with something approaching a wry little smile, "your father would have said no harm was done."

Claire softened. "No harm would have been done," she said, "and it would have been such a wonderful happening for me. Just something glamorous, I think. That's all. Girls of twelve don't disturb so easily. It's the early part I want to know about. They never talked about it to me. Only recently, when I asked. They said you left me flat. Is that what you did?" *Without a backward glance*, Aunt Marcia had said.

Momentarily, June's face closed, hardened. She seemed to take herself in hand, as though she had fought a battle with anger, and won. "Because you were so young, and because your father's work took him all over the world, in my naïveté I thought I could have you here with me. I really believed that, Claire. I tried to go back to get you, but you'd been made a Ward of Court. Then I thought I would be able to have you at least a part of the time. I was totally thrown by the decision the judge and your father made."

"Why did they do it?"

"I'd run off with a penniless foreigner of twenty when I was twenty-five and should have known better how to behave. He, Manuel, had not even been able to finish college because his father died and he had a great cluster of brothers and sisters all much younger than himself to look after, not to mention his mother. In an English court it sounded a bad background for an English child. I couldn't bring the judge here to see Manuel and how he lived."

"Am I permitted to ask what Manuel thought of Father keeping me in England?" Claire asked.

"He was saddened. He didn't understand. He kept saying: 'You cannot part a baby from her mother, no matter what the mother has done.' "

Moved in spite of herself, but still with that tightness in her, Claire's mind flashed back to the night when Manuel had thrown Ricardo and herself out of the farmhouse. "The English think of Spaniards as bad husbands," she said. "Unfaithful. Father and the judge might have thought Manuel would go off with another woman and leave you without support."

"Your father was faithful to me," Juanita Manzales flashed, and suddenly there was a new side to her that Claire had not suspected. "Faithful and cold and hard and totally unyielding. You can't deny that, Claire. As his daughter you must have experienced it."

The practiced loyalty of years hardened to form a block to stem what was perhaps deserved betrayal.

"I should have gone with Manuel to England and faced up to your father. It's too late," June lamented. "You've wanted to find me, but now that you have, you can't forgive. It's going to be a long road back, but so long as you don't hate me, it is possible to make the journey, Claire . . . my daughter." Her gray eyes were wide and pleading.

"I don't hate you," said Claire. "It's just that our relationship seems doomed. You know what I mean. I'm sure you know what I mean. Ricardo will have told you."

June smiled indulgently. "That he loves you? My dear, how long have you known him? A few days? A few days in a new, glamorous place. A handsome young man with a fast car. And for him, a pretty, pale English girl." She put a hand over Claire's. "Of course it's enough to turn the heads of both of you. Of course it's totally understandable. But it's not a good enough reason for ruining the lives of other people," she pointed out soberly. "It really is not. One day you'll wake up and find yourself out of love with this handsome, and may I say very willful young man, and you'll simply float off back home, but there'll be no turning back for the others. The damage will have been done."

"Did anyone say that to you when you fell in

love with Manuel while on vacation in Scotland?"

The two women stared at each other, two sets of suddenly bleak gray eyes in white faces. June seemed shaken, unable to go on. She seemed to have shrunk behind the staring eyes.

* * * *

At last Claire asked: "Would you tell me why you left Manuel?"

"I felt I could not be torn apart any more. I love Ricardo, and I love Manuel. But something has to be done, or we'll all be lost. I told Manuel I would return when Ricardo decided to do what he must do."

"Marry Rosita?"

"Claire," she cried despairingly, "you're English. So much more English that I am, now. You can't understand the Spanish way, Ricardo was seeing a lot of Rosita—"

"I know about it. Teresa told me."

They sat in silence. A little later June said: "Spaniards—not just Spaniards—many men, and your own father was one of them, Claire, sometimes feel very strongly about their beloved daughters. And anyway, it would be difficult for you to understand the way things are done in Spain. The girls don't have so much freedom, so if a girl goes out a lot with a young man without a chaperone, it's thought, and expected, that she'll marry him."

"So you're willing to sacrifice Ricardo to this girl? You, personally?" Claire asked. She picked at the edge of a cushion, avoiding her mother's eyes. "You see, I do know all about this. I know the girl's crippled."

"It's very sad. Perhaps if she could marry Ricardo—well, when a person is happy she is more likely to make an effort," June said, avoiding Claire's eyes.

Something that might be guilt in her manner galvanized Claire into a protest. "Teresa says she's not even a nice girl."

"It's not for Teresa to say," June replied sharply. "Ricardo liked her well enough before she was crippled." Another silence while the indisputable facts sank in.

"Is this part of the story? Why you left Manuel?"

June nodded. "That afternoon I had had a telephone call from Miranda, our hostess, saying she was in the area and wished to call and see us. I was expecting her when Rosita's father arrived. He said he'd heard Manuel had at last sold two properties. The hotel and one of the big villas. He said I must tell Manuel that unless Ricardo makes up his mind to marry Rosita he will withhold the water from these properties. That means the sales won't go through. We can't live without water, Claire. If Manuel doesn't sell these properties then we'll starve. All his money is sunk into his developments. All of it. And the economic situation has been so bad no one has been buying."

"Starve?" Claire echoed incredulously. "Why can't Manuel go to work somewhere?" She saw June's look of astonishment and added defensively: "Other people do. For that matter, why can't you work?" She seemed to grow stronger with her anger, or as June lost ground. "Forgive me for being blunt, but it seems to me that a temporary setback in the family's standards doesn't compare with the sort of disaster you're trying to inflict on Ricardo. Some day a solution will be found to this water problem. I think it's diabolical that one man should have the town in the palm of his hand. Why doesn't someone do something about that?"

June said: "It isn't just that. There are the boys. Manuel's responsible for Josefina too, and for Leop—"

"No."

"Yes, for Leopoldo's work. Yes, yes, Leopoldo and Manuel must work together."

"No. They don't have to," Claire said passionately. "Leopoldo's a builder. He can work for anyone. So can Teresa. She doesn't have to have a boutique set up for her by Manuel. She hasn't stood on her own feet because she hasn't had to, but I'm sure she can. Isn't it really that Manuel hasn't wanted the family to be independent?"

June sighed sharply. "There's so much you don't know. So much you don't understand."

"Go on. Señora Cervera came in her car, and you decided to run away with her to Tangier? To freeze Manuel into forcing Ricardo to do this diabolical thing?" She hung on June's answer, not wanting the harsh facts she was putting into words to be true.

"It was like that," said June, looking drained. "I telephoned Manuel at the office and told him of Pascual's threat. He wouldn't believe it at first. Then he said he'd go off to Granada to have another try to raise some money, but due to the economic situation he knew he had virtually no hope. I knew he wouldn't come home and neither would he go straight to Granada because it was too

late for the banks. They would all be closed. I
knew he'd go to the *finca*—that's a farm we have in
the hills where he always goes when he's worried.
When he wants to be alone."

Claire felt her color rise and glanced away. So
that was why Manuel had gone to the *finca*! For
the same reason Ricardo went there. Was that
what Ricardo had meant when he said the old
man, Raphael, who looked after the farm, didn't
tell tales? Manuel might not like Ricardo using the
house without permission.

"I had time to pack," June was saying. "I've
been torn to ribbons over this issue, Claire. I felt I
couldn't take any more. I had to force Manuel to
help himself. I left a note saying I'd return when
Manuel had made Ricardo see reason. I cannot
have the family suffer so for Ricardo's indiscre-
tions."

Claire said bitterly: "I thought—because you
were my mother—I thought you had left because
you couldn't bear to see Manuel force Ricardo into
this marriage."

June looked startled, shaken, then her eyes
filled again with tears. Claire turned away, not
wanting to see how she had hurt her. At the same
time her mind was racing. Why did Manuel want
money if it would not buy water? She brushed a
hand across her damp forehead. Anger, distress,
had taken too much of her small store of strength.
Her body felt a dead weight against the velvet
cushions. And yet, a sort of second wind pushed
her along.

"You mean, Manuel wanted money to live on?"
she asked. "You mean he was prepared to string
this thing out, for Ricardo's sake, living off

borrowed money in a fool's paradise? Is Manuel so short of cash?" She wanted to say: *Is he so soft with Ricardo? Are you so hard?*

"It's all so complicated," said June, biting her lips.

"Is this man Pascual a friend of yours?" Teresa had said the family grew close during the time Rosita was very ill.

"A friend?" June's mouth turned down bitterly. "The families have been feuding for generations, until Manuel foolishly saw a chance to make up."

"I don't understand it," said Claire. She took a tissue and wiped her face. "I don't understand how you can sacrifice Ricardo. I'm certain there must be a way out. Can't water be carted from somewhere? Can't a deputation from the town go to Pascual and persuade him? Can—" She stopped as she saw her mother's face crumpling.

"I have to tell you," June said, her voice trembling. "I must tell you the whole story. It—" she hesitated, then said in a rush, "it has to do with Manuel's essential goodness. There was this feud, a very long time ago, between Manuel's great-grandfather and Pascual's grandfather. The families always kept apart until Ricardo started going out with Rosita. If he hadn't done that—Well, it's too late," she commented bitterly. "Manuel was halfway through building this hotel and the new complex of houses that's up behind the almond grove, when he ran out of money. Prices of materials had risen and anyway, he'd overstepped himself by building the hotel. He thought it would be a very good investment, but in the end it turned out to be not quite big enough for the people who showed interest. He'd fallen between two stools—too big for a house, not big enough for a hotel. This man who wants to buy it now intends to use it as a club. Manuel was going to the bank to borrow the money to finish. It was just at the start of the recession we've been having, but the banks would have loaned to him at that time.

"Pascual heard about it. Men talk in bars, you know. The town's small and everyone, anyway, is interested in the Manzales. He came to Manuel one night in a bar and offered to loan the money. It was before Rosita's accident."

"Yet they had never been friends? Manuel borrowed money from such a man? An enemy?" Claire asked incredulously.

"He saw an opportunity to mend a long-standing rift. Manuel's like that. You don't know my husband, Claire," June said earnestly. "He's a good man. An honest and kindly man. He never did believe that this family feud was any of his affair and he took the first opportunity he saw to mend it. If he'd turned Pascual's offer down, the man would have been insulted, and the rift would have remained. Manuel's normal farsightedness was blunted by the love he has for his fellow men, Claire. He was not to know that at heart Fernando Pascual was wicked."

"And you want Ricardo married to the daughter of this man?" Claire demanded to know, newly outraged, newly despairing.

"It's not that anyone wants him to marry Rosita," June replied, her tortured eyes on Claire's. "What Pascual said to me the day I left was not only that he'll withhold the water. He also threatened to foreclose. And that means Manuel, who is unable to pay, will go to prison."

"Prison!" Claire exclaimed incredulously. "He wouldn't go to prison! Pascual could sue him, and his assets might be confiscated."

"The family land! The land Manuel's father left to him as a safeguard for the family!"

Claire said gently: "Manuel would sell the land eventually. He would sell houses built on the land." She found herself smiling. "Nineteen years as the sheltered wife of a patriarchal Spaniard has made you a little unworldly, hasn't it? What about your own villa? Pascual couldn't cut off your water without cutting off other people's. So you could sell that."

June's face was marble white. "Yes," she said quietly. "I hadn't thought. We could sell my home."

Claire's heart contracted. For some little time an idea had been nibbling at the back of her mind. There was her father's house in Surrey that was in the process of being sold for what seemed an inordinately large sum. A sum of money for which, certainly at the moment, she had no need. Then suddenly in her mind's eye there was Aunt Marcia's warning voice. *Life is ridiculous, I know, but don't let it be as ridiculous as that.* She said, her voice a little out of control as a sort of panic took her in its grip: "Better to sell your villa than ruin Ricardo's life."

"Yes. Y-yes. Until you put it—until you—" June's voice broke. When she began again the words were strained: "I hadn't thought it ruined— before."

"My coming has changed things."

June nodded. "I suppose you always have to pay," she said, still in that strained voice. "Either in this world or the next. Perhaps it's better to get it over with." She smiled faintly. "I could wish the rules were a little more clear at the outset. It's right, of course, that you, my daughter, should be the implement of justice. Or is it revenge? I don't mean that personally," she added in a detached voice. "It's as far out of your hands as it is of mine. We're merely the instruments of Fate. It's just that—" June's voice broke again, "we do try, so hard, to do what's right. It doesn't seem fair that people have to go to the end of the road before finding they were wrong all the time. And then take the punishment."

Claire's right hand went automatically to the left, her finger tips touching the skin where the ring had been. She had wished, and the wish was coming true. June's hold was loosening on the trap gripping Ricardo's life. She had not counted on herself being sick to the heart of her at the result. She looked round the walls of the strange and exotic room. At the door-leaves with knot work embedded mosaic-wise between pieces of wood. At the dark rafters in the ceiling and the corbels that must surely be a medieval survival.

Someone had said to her once, or perhaps she had read it somewhere, that you must be careful with wishes, for they may come true. You cannot wish disaster away, Claire thought, already with despair in her heart, for disaster is not an entity in itself. Its coming is a gradual process. All along the line the mistakes had piled up, implementing many happenings, many people. June's leaving her baby; Ricardo's involvement with the girl from a family that had feuded for generations with his own; Manuel's shortsighted, ill-reasoned attempt at peacemaking; her own father and his stiff-necked judge who could not look into a woman's heart. And now the reckoning had come.

"How much money does Manuel owe Pascual?" she asked bleakly.

"I don't know exactly. Too much."

"I have some. Father left me all he had. His savings, and the house. Its sale is going through now. I get quite an inflated price for it because of its being in a desirable position on a village green." She saw the look of astonishment on June's face, saw the tears spill over to run down her cheeks. Resolutely, she turned her face away. She did not want her mother's thanks. She was not doing it for her. She was doing it for herself and Ricardo. Suddenly Aunt Marcia's face, fiercely indignant, seemed to be everywhere, and her voice, echoing: *What on earth has your mother done to deserve . . .*

June's humble, trembling words came through: ". . . to be so rewarded by you?" and she realized it had not been Marcia's voice at all. Claire turned to look at June. To look at herself twenty years on. She wanted to shout: "Nothing! Nothing! You don't deserve it. I'm doing this for myself." But the words did not come, as they should not, because somewhere hidden behind the confusion of emotionalism that stormed within her, there was a tiny bit of truth groping to get through. She thought of the photographs in the hall of June's villa. June looking down at the babies with her eyes full of love and tenderness. Once upon a time, because human beings don't change so much or so quickly, before her life was split down the center, Juanita Manzales must have looked at her like that. Perhaps June's ex-husband's money would do something towards making up to her for what he had withheld.

"It's a sort of revenge," Claire said bleakly, wondering if, beyond the grave, her father heard.

"I don't understand."

"No. It doesn't matter." Treachery should go unmarked. She put a hand to her head. "I think I should go back to bed, only I don't think I can get there. It's all been rather too much."

SIXTEEN

Claire had never met anyone quite like Miranda Cervera. Incomparably handsome, there was a formidable quality about her that excluded beauty. Having deposited the breakfast tray on the table at Claire's bedside, she seated herself by the window and lit a cigarette. "Your mother's gone out to buy some gifts to take home," she said. "Wherever Juanita goes, she returns laden with presents. And she will expect presents from you."

Claire gave her a sharp look. Señora Cervera's profile was etched against the clear desert light, her dark eyes hooded, her blue-black hair drawn back with a severity that only a woman supremely confident of her looks would adopt. She drew slowly at her cigarette and blew the smoke out in a spiral. Its aromatic scent drifted back into the room. "Was that a loaded remark?" Claire asked.

"Heavily loaded. Yes."

"June's told you—"

Her hostess cut in. "It would make your mother very happy if you'd call her Juanita, just for a while until you form the sort of relationship that will allow you to call her Mother." Claire glared at the Spanish woman. Señora Cervera looked back at her with tranquillity, and slowly indignation gave way to faint surprise and a curious feeling of acceptance. "You see," said her mother's friend, speaking gently, "I'm a good deal older, my dear, and, while age doesn't necessarily bring wisdom, it does give one a background picture so that it's easier to place the bits of the jigsaw. Especially," she added dryly, "other people's jigsaws."

"All right. I take the bit about the new relationship. It isn't so easy, you know."

"Nothing worth doing is easy."

"No. I dare say not. So you think I was a fool to offer to help Manuel out?"

"No." A piece of ash fell on the Señora's immaculate caftan and she flicked it away. "Unashamedly behind your mother's back, I'm saying you should understand the family will give back only in their own way."

Claire poured the coffee from its little silver jug. She pushed the toast aside. "What do you mean?"

"I've no doubt you think of yourself as a stranger, but the Manzales family, from old Josefina to little Vicente, will think of you as family. They'll not look upon this very generous offer for the sacrifice it is. They'll think merely that a member of their family has miraculously, by the good graces of the Holy Virgin, been empowered to help. I want to be sure you understand the situation before you part with your cash, my dear. No doubt they told you Manuel has tried to patch up a long-standing family fued. But feuding is the lifeblood of the Spaniard. Manuel may consider himself a visionary, and certainly he's an exceptionally good man, but he's only a pin-point in the history of the Spanish people. Withholding the water for Manuel's developments is merely a straw Pascual has grasped to aid him in carrying on the family quarrel that has been in his blood so long there's no getting rid of it."

"But Pascual wants Ricardo to marry Rosita," Claire cried in bewilderment. "If what you say is true, what does this mean?"

"Only that she shall have a husband," replied her hostess tartly. "Rosita has no future, so her father must dredge up something from the past. Frankly, and I hope you won't think I am being uncharitable, I think Rosita is using her situation to manipulate Ricardo. Of course, she may feel it's the only way she will get him. Once she's safely married there is always the possibility she may make an effort to walk again. I had a Red Cross job during the war and one thing I learned was that the mind, the nervous system and the spine are inextricably tied up together. I've seen people walking again literally because they want to walk. And I've seen people sitting in wheelchairs because it's easier."

Teresa had said something like that. And had not the thought been in Juanita's mind, for she had hinted at the same thing when she was telling Claire how she came to leave Manuel? Blindly angry, Claire tried to tell herself that even three assumptions did not make a truth. She had not met Rosita. She must not judge her. And the unwelcome but undeniable fact was that the girl was certainly in a cripple's chair now.

Miranda Cervera lifted her head, listening. "Oh! I think I hear Juanita. She's back early." She rose. "I hope I've given you food for thought. Don't let it bother you, though. You may recall some of it some time and find it useful. Only remember to ask yourself, when you purchase Ricardo, if he's worth the price you pay."

Claire flushed scarlet. "You're pretty blunt."

"It's that sort of situation."

"And you think he's not worth it?"

"I think he's worth a great deal," Miranda Cervera broke in gently, "but I am not doing the paying. You made this very generous decision during a time of emotional stress and when you weren't even well."

"I'll tell you why I've done it."

"You don't need to. Perhaps you heard the quarrel between Ricardo and Juanita the night Ricardo left? It occurred on the balcony directly below your window."

Claire shook her head. "Only a few words."

"When I heard Ricardo say: 'You have not lost Claire and you need not, if you don't do this monstrous thing to her,' I knew immediately. I don't know whether Ricardo has gone home to marry this girl, or whether he's gone to fight with Manuel, but whatever's going on, don't think you've solved the whole problem by waving your check book."

June came in with her arms full of parcels. She flung them down on the bed. "You haven't eaten your breakfast!"

Their hostess said indulgently: "I've been

telling Claire that you buy presents for everyone, all the time."

"And why not? Is that not what money's for? Claire, my darling, I can't wait to see how these suit you. A gold caftan for dressing up and a cotton one for wearing around the villa."

"You shouldn't be spending all this money on me, Juanita." It was, after all, only a name and it slid easily past the block in her throat that Claire had thought would strangle it. If either of the older women noticed, they showed no sign.

"But of course I shall," Juanita cried. "At last I have a daughter and I must make a fuss of her." There were leather belts for the boys; a painted leather cushion for Teresa; an enormous caftan for Josefina; two black lace mantillas for the maids.

"Are you going home then?" Claire asked.

"I've telephoned Manuel. He's coming for us, just as soon as you're well enough."

"Did you tell him—?"

"No. That's for you. I can ask Manuel exactly how much money is involved, then you will make your very kind offer. But all that matters now is that you should get quickly well again. Of course there are splendid things for you to see here—the Sultan's Palace, the snake charmers, the belly dancers, the bazaars. We could drive you to the Atlas Mountains to fill your lungs with air . . ."

Claire was touched by Juanita's happiness, her sweet acceptance of Fate's quixotic reversals, but she was afraid. She had to write to Aunt Marcia. Her aunt, she knew, would fight to the last ditch to stop her spending her money to help Manuel. And she wanted to go back to Spain quickly, because she was afraid of what might be happening there. Señora Cervera had described Ricardo as willful. . . .

That afternoon, dressed fetchingly in the new cotton caftan her mother had so lovingly chosen for her, sitting at the Chinese desk in the absent Señor Cervera's study, Claire penned the letter to Aunt Marcia. *I know you will not agree . . . prepared even for violent opposition . . . see no reason to bear a grudge against Juanita . . . faults on both sides . . .* She crossed out the name Juanita and wrote in June, then put Juanita back again. It took five drafts before the letter was ready. Claire gave it to one of the servants to post. In the afternoon she relaxed on a comfortable sofa of painted leather that the servants carried into the courtyard. She wanted to rest and grow strong quickly.

"But you must see something of Morocco," Juanita protested. "It's terrible to come here and see only the inside of walls."

"Such beautiful walls are worth a journey in themselves."

Manuel was to bring the big Mercedes to Algeciras and come over to Tangier on the hydrofoil. The Cervera car would meet him and bring him to the house. Claire stayed in her room, for the reunion between Manuel and Jaunita was something she had not wanted to witness. She was standing at the window looking out on the cascading roofs and across to the minaret, stark against the unreal blueness of the Eastern sky when her hostess came to fetch her. This afternoon she was dressed gorgeously in bright red with gold embroidery, and her painted toenails peeped out of gold slippers. She said:

"You will promise me to come back, Claire, before I allow you to go."

Claire smiled. "I'd love to come back. You've been so very good to me, and I'm a complete stranger to you."

Miranda Cervera brushed her gratitude aside. "Your mother, until I met you, was the most vulnerable person I'd ever met. We're good for each other. She leans on me, and she softens me. Let's say I give her strength, and I take some of her sweetness in return. Be gentle with your mother, Claire. You, too, are strong, but you have what she has, a soft and vulnerable centre. You could be very badly hurt, and I want you to promise me that if this happens you'll come back here, for your mother won't be able to do anything for you. She'll suffer for you, but she won't be able to help." A quiver of fear went through Claire. "I wish you luck, my dear," Miranda Cervera said gently. She glanced down at Claire's hand. "You're wearing a ring."

Claire flushed "It's nothing. Just from the bazaar. It has no value."

"It's very pretty. But I should put it away if I were you."

"Why?"

"Because you've been fingering it all the time I've been talking to you. Your mother will notice and ask you about it and maybe suspect, for you're very transparent, you know. I'd hide it, if I were you, until your problems are resolved."

Manuel and Juanita were waiting in the courtyard. Manuel descended upon Claire like a benevolent storm, arms held wide. "The little

Claire! You found your mother." Having embraced her fondly, he stood back to admire the two of them together. His women, Claire thought, amused. His own. Manuel strutted like a peacock again. Neither by word nor sign did he mention his reason for being here, and neither did Juanita explain her reversal or show any embarrassment at being led home. She was clearly anxious to go.

They said good-bye to their hostess and left by a barred gate in a wall where a sentry stood on guard. The big American car, fitting the street like a glove, crept away silently through the medina and so out into the wider streets of the town. The fronds of the palms that lined the waterfront were blowing, but the Straits of Gibraltar, thankfully, seemed calm enough. They went on board the hydrofoil and settled down together in the high-backed seats of the lounge, Manuel fussing anxiously, checking that Claire was comfortable, that she felt well, holding Juanita's arm tightly all the while in his. And Juanita now had a cherished air; she would never have looked like this with my father, Claire thought sadly. Never. It had not been in John Richardson to make a woman blossom the way Juanita blossomed beneath the shining star of Manuel's personality, girded and lifted by the exuberance of his love.

Whatever the rights and wrongs of the situation, the deprivation to Juanita and to her self for loss of their early relationship, whatever the suffering inflicted on her father, Claire sensed already that her mother had been right to leave.

Perhaps her going had been a spiritual trial for John; a testing time. That he had failed the test was another matter and out of their hands.

Within moments the hydrofoil rose on its skis and sped out into the Mediterranean leaving the gray, rocky hills of Africa behind. Ahead lay the grand and spectacular Rock of Gibraltar, and westward, the greener hills of Spain. Claire, looking in her basket for a tissue, saw her purse and temptation overtook her with a longing to see the ring again. She opened the purse carefully. It was still there, glowing ruby red among the Spanish coins. She touched the stone superstitiously, and made a little wish.

As the big car purred towards Malaga, Claire remembered Juanita's little Fiat parked beneath some rowan trees in the street outside the hotel. But "Ricardo has collected it," Manuel assured her. Her belongings also had been collected, and the hotel bill paid. They went to the school to fetch the boys.

"Can you imagine taking English children out of school to welcome you home?" And after such a peccadillo, too, Claire thought dryly.

Juanita only said: "It's what I want for them. A sense of the family's unity. To feel a part of the family and share everything that happens." Juanita went into the school and they emerged together.

"Hello, my sister Claire," cried Juan jubilantly. This time he kissed her on either cheek, whispering in her ear: "We're both very, very sorry." Then: "You've been ill. We'll look after you and make you better."

"I'll bring you toast in bed," volunteered Vicente shyly, his eyes wide with apprehension as he searched Claire's face for signs that they were forgiven. Claire kissed them both, told them they were bad boys, that she was quite, quite better, and bygones were bygones.

It was early evening when they arrived at the villa on the hill. The sun was dropping towards the horizon but the air was very warm. Up in her room Claire took the ring from her basket and slipped it on her finger, turning it in the last rays of the setting sun. For a bazaar bauble it was beautiful indeed. She held it up to the light. The metal did look extraordinarily like platinum or white gold. What if it had been stolen? She wrapped the ring in tissue and put it carefully back in her purse. When she came down dressed in her new gold caftan and wearing the gold shoes Ricardo had given her, the garden was bathed in perfume brought on the evening breeze from the almond trees on the hillside opposite. Someone had switched on a light at the end of the pool and the two marble lions glowered benevolently across the water. Shadows shifted prettily beneath the big palm. Claire was met in the hall by a smiling Oliva. Everyone was happy now Juanita was home.

Manuel came through from the kitchen, his magnificent head high, a bottle of champagne embedded in an ice bucket held triumphantly aloft.

The boys came out of the pool. They stood side by side on the grass, their slim, wet bodies shining in the light from the verandah. They looked interestedly at the bottle. "Why are we having that, Papa?" Vicente asked.

"Because your mother has returned, and there's something else. I have news for you."

Juanita came down the stairs. She, too, was wearing a caftan she had bought in Tangier. "Do you like the new look of your ladies, Manuel?"

He held both arms wide, extravagantly. "I could eat you."

"Eat them?" The boys exchanged delighted glances, then laughed aloud together.

"What's the good news, Manuel?" Juanita asked.

"I've sold a house. And the hotel." He watched their faces, waiting for their reaction. Juanita looked puzzled. Claire blinked. Manuel slapped his knee, enjoying the surprise he had engendered.

"But there's no—water—"

"Fernando has given us the water," Manuel roared. "They're really sold now." Juanita flashed a nervous glance at Claire, then looked away. Claire could not look at Manuel. "Fernando is a Christian at heart," Manuel went on generously. Claire felt her eyes drawn to Juanita's face. Juanita was looking at her shoes. Footsteps sounded in the hall and Claire swung around. Ricardo? But it was Leopoldo and Teresa who came to join them on the verandah.

"Hello, everybody." Leopoldo bent to kiss Claire's hand. "I heard my brother had gone to bring you and Juanita back." Teresa ran to Juanita, embracing her lovingly. Claire found herself glancing obsessively towards the door.

Where was Ricardo? "Hello, Juanita, my dear," Leopoldo was saying. He kissed her on both cheeks. "It looks as though I'm just in time." Oliva was coming with a tray of glasses. "Manuel is about to open a bottle of champagne?"

"We're celebrating, Leopoldo," Juanita explained. "Fernando has released the water for the house and the hotel." Still she avoided Claire's eyes.

Leopoldo said, shifting uncomfortably from one foot to the other: "I think there may be something Ricardo hasn't yet told us. I heard it in the town today."

They all looked up at him. Teresa, too, seemed uncomfortable. Claire was conscious of Juanita's quick inrush of breath.

"What did you hear?" Manuel asked.

Claire felt it coming, like a creeping serpent. Felt the cold of what she had feared closing around her heart. "Ricardo is to marry Rosita, after all. They've seen Father Emmanuel today," Leopoldo told them, "and it's all arranged. I think Ricardo must have told Pascual when he returned from Tangier." Leopoldo looked around at the silent faces. "What else could be the cause of Fernando allowing Manuel to have the water?"

Claire's stricken eyes met the gray ones opposite. "What did you say to Ricardo that night he left Tangier? You were quarreling." She tried to keep the anger, the hurt, the sharp accusations out of her voice but they came like a whiplash, jerking at the new, frail bond between herself and her mother.

Juanita looked close to tears. "Of course he had

to marry this girl," she cried in anguish, "otherwise Manuel is never going to be free of Fernando Pascual." She ran to Claire and knelt down by the sofa, looking up into her face. "Claire, darling, it was wonderful and generous of you to offer the money, but it would have been only a temporary measure. A patching. It would not have solved the problem at the root. Ricardo *has* to marry Rosita. It's the only way."

"You knew this?" asked Claire angrily. "You knew it, even when you were pretending I could save him with my inheritance?"

Juanita looked distraught. "I was pretending to myself, not to you. I tried to convince myself that it would work. But it would not. I have to face the fact now that it would not. Claire, please, darling, try to accept it. Ricardo must do what's expected of him. It is right, in a way you don't understand, that he should marry Rosita."

Claire stared at the bottle of champagne until her eyes seemed to burn in their sockets. Juanita flung both arms around her and wept. The others stood in a small half-circle, uncomfortable, silent.

"Please say something," Juanita beseeched her. "What are you thinking, Claire?"

She was thinking of what Miranda Cervera had said. "Your mother will suffer for you, but she won't be able to help." Claire looked bleakly into Juanita Manzales's tortured eyes, seeing her as a stranger whose loyalties were for the family she had built up since leaving her English child. Whose whole world was a new edifice that could not contain the past. Claire turned away to hide the anguish and met dawning hostility in Juan's puzzled eyes. Vicente came forward to put his arms around his mother, his young face concerned. His comforting words were spoken in Spanish. Then Juan spoke sharply, also in Spanish. Anger whipped in Manuel's eyes, for whom Claire did not know, then Leopoldo, his surprisingly blond head high, unleashed a tirade on Manuel and Manuel flashed back at him. Juan pulled his mother to her feet. She turned a torrent of foreign rhetoric on Leopoldo. Then they were all shouting at once and the air was vibrant with the storm Claire had unleashed.

She rose. As if they saw her intention in her face, suddenly they calmed. They all looked at her apologetically, six Spaniards setting aside their Spanish passion for a moment to recognize the presence of an English girl.

Claire addressed her mother directly. "Did you tell Ricardo, in Tangier, that Pascual was blackmailing you into this arranged marriage? Is that why Ricardo left and came back to make the arrangements to marry Rosita?"

"I had to tell him. It was the only way."

"Of course. It's a pity, though, for now that he knows he was blackmailed into it, the marriage doesn't have the remotest chance of success." The silence in the room was intense. Claire heaved an enormous sigh. "Let's drink to the prosperity of the Manzales family," she suggested. She looked up at Manuel, emotionally drained, her voice sounding like a thin echo of itself. "I told Juanita I would loan you my inheritance to help you out, but it's true it was only half a solution. And I was loaning it for the wrong reasons. Besides, it would have caused no end of trouble at home. Let's have this little celebration; then I'll go. I seem to have made rather a mess of things. Some time, when your problems are all behind you, I'll come back and perhaps we can try again."

SEVENTEEN

Claire packed in the quiet of early morning. Outside, the sun, a scarlet ball, lifted itself slowly from a silver abyss between sea and sky. The little fishing boats were on their way. She clipped down the lid of her suitcase, took her jacket out of the wardrobe, laid her handbag beside it then sat down on the covered seat by the window to wait for the villa's stirring. Last night there had been no protestations about her going. It was as though her departure was a firecracker no one dared touch. They were gentle with her, and loving. They watched her face anxiously when they thought she was not looking, and hid their guilt as best they could. It would have been easy enough to run away in the night but she was too tired, too sick at heart to run. Besides, she had done a fair job of facing up to inevitabilities and she was fairly confident she could continue with a calm façade at least until she was clear of the villa. She had a half-formed plan to go to Malaga, hire a car and drive herself slowly back to England, filling in the time until she felt confident that she could face her relatives with a smile. For she would have to learn to smile about this fiasco and adopt some sort of humorous defense against the inevitable "I told you so" that would be Aunt Marcia's retort.

This morning Claire wore the ring. As I will always wear it, she thought, twisting the stone so that the facets caught the light. And she would resist the temptation to get it appraised. She had driven into the back of her mind the nagging suspicions about its value. What could she do about a theft that may have taken place in a North African town? She knew now the ring itself was not made of silver. White gold? Platinum? It had a pale silvery luster that bore no relation to silver or the impermanent glitter of baser metals. The stone was a blazing ruby red in the morning light. It was to be her keepsake in memory of a dream. She held it against her cheek, blinking away the tears.

After a while, with time hanging heavily, she went downstairs. She walked swiftly past the mother-and-child photographs with eyes turned resolutely away. The doors leading to the verandah were closed but not locked. She opened them and wandered across the coarse-bladed, emerald green grass to the swimming pool. Perfume from the blossom-girded hill drifted in. Looking back at the pretty villa she thought bitterly: My going is the end of this. I can never come back. What doesn't work today won't work tomorrow. I had my chance, and I made a mess of it.

Perhaps, after all, she should take the coward's way out and go before anyone woke up. Could she carry her bag as far as the coast road where she might thumb a lift to the station? You can do anything you want to, if you really want, she said to herself.

She went back up the stairs. A door opened and Juanita came out. She wore a pretty pale blue housecoat. Her face was soft with sleep but when she saw Claire, and beyond her the suitcase on the floor, she spoke sharply, nervously: "You're up early."

"Yes, I'm ready to go. I'm only waiting to say good-bye."

Juanita's eyes darkened. "You can't go," she protested. "Not like this."

Claire hardened her heart. "I said last night I was going. You didn't say anything then."

"We thought you'd feel differently this morning."

"Is it possible for you to drive me to the station? Or would you phone for a taxi? Perhaps could I borrow your car? I'd really rather leave before Manuel wakes. *Please*, Juanita." She could not look at her mother. Suddenly feeling the tears close, she hurried back into her bedroom and slung her bag over her shoulder. But Juanita had followed her in. She said: "Let's have a talk, dear."

"No. No, I'm sorry. Nothing can come of it." Claire's left hand lay on the back of a small chair. Juanita's eyes rested on the ring, dilated, lifted to meet Claire's, then returned to the ring. "Where did you get that?"

"From the bazaar in Tangier."

"Oh, no. Oh no!" Juanita was deeply distressed. "You're lying."

Claire flushed angrily. "It was bought from a street-seller."

"By you?"

"By a—a friend."

Juanita came closer, her eyes riveted on the ring. She lifted Claire's fingers, looked closely at the ring, then looked back into Claire's now apprehensive face. "That," said Juanita, touching the stone, "in case you really don't know, is an Alexandrite. A rare and very valuable stone. The ring came from Russia with one of Manuel's ancestors who was married to a White Russian."

"Oh!" said Claire faintly.

Juanita looked at her oddly, as though waiting for a confession, and when Claire did not go on, continued: "They had a narrow escape during the revolution and superstitiously attributed their salvation to the ring. It's been known as a lucky ring ever since. The family says that you may wish on it and . . ." Juanita's shadowed, troubled eyes met Claire's and her voice trailed away.

"And all your wishes will come true," Claire finished softly, her eyes alight.

Juanita's face was twisted with anguish. "You can't keep it, my dear."

"But Ricardo gave it to me."

"He had no right. No right at all. Josefina gave him this special ring for Rosita. It's Rosita who needs wishes to come true. You're fit and well. You have everything. It was not Ricardo's ring to give to you. It belongs to Manuel, Claire, don't you understand? It belongs to the head of the family and it was given for Rosita—and for a very special reason. There are miracles, you know. There are miracles," Juanita repeated in anguish. "Josefina thought Rosita might wish for a miracle, and then try hard to make it come true—if she had the ring, I mean."

Claire's forefinger tightened around the ring. They stood in silence. Juanita's distress seemed to come from another world of which Claire had no part. A distress that could not touch her. It was as though a haunting spell had taken possession of her now. An exquisite enchantment. "If this ring got an ancestor out of the Russian revolution, then perhaps it will get Ricardo out of this terrible situation," she said.

"I wish you had not said that. I do wish you had not. Please give the ring to me. I don't want Manuel to see it." Tentatively, Juanita held out her hand. "Please give it to me, darling. Please. I'll give it back to Ricardo."

Claire found herself saying: "You, of all people, should understand. How long did it take you to fall in love with Manuel?"

"Don't ask me those questions. Please don't ask," Juanita looked afraid.

"I have a right to ask. How long did it take you to fall in love with him?"

Juanita clutched her gown around her. Her eyes were enormous.

"Go on. Tell me."

"In an instant, if you must know. I saw him walking towards me, in the street, with a friend of your father's."

"And I," Claire told her, "I fell in love with Ricardo as he crossed the square down there in the town."

Juanita turned away as though unable to look her daughter in the eyes. Then, swinging back she said placatingly: "He won't be so tied. He'll give Rosita his name, but he will be more free than you might think. It's different here for a man, Claire."

"Are you offering me a—what would you call it—a liaison with Ricardo? You—my mother?"

"No. No, of course not. But if you love Ricardo you will want to know that his life will not be—narrowed. That he won't be cornered, as you might say."

Claire told her mother bleakly, "I want to return to the fact that there isn't one rule for you and one for me. You thought you had a right to the man you fell in love with. You didn't think about Father and me."

Juanita burst into tears. "I know. I did it at your expense. Don't think I haven't lived with that guilt for nineteen years. No one gets away scot-free, Claire. Believe me. If you take Ricardo from Rosita at the expense of my family, you will not get away scot-free."

Claire's head was spinning: "I'm not giving this ring to you or Manuel. I am going to take it to Ricardo because he gave it to me. I'll ask him if he wants it back." And then, with crushing despair, she remembered her promise to Pascual not to see Ricardo. Did two wrongs make a right? And was it not all over? Inevitably, all over? Pascual would have told Ricardo about her promise. And Juanita had blackmailed him into freeing Manuel of his debt. There was no turning back. She handed the ring to her mother. "Okay," she said, her voice breaking. "You've won."

Juanita took the girl tenderly in her arms and they wept together. "You won't run away? You have a family here," Juanita said when the emotional moment was over. "We all love you. Let me try to make up."

Even that! Claire said brokenly: "I'll try to develop a sense of humor. Help me, Juanita. Please help me . . ."

* * * *

Next week the sale of Manuel's hotel would be complete. So there was to be a party in it to celebrate Ricardo's engagement to Rosita. Since her return from Africa, Claire had not seen Ricardo. Teresa said he was helping Raphael up at the *finca*. At the villa, no one talked about him but Claire was certain the various members of the family met him in the town. Tonight, she was expected to do her duty as Juanita's daughter and shake hands with the new sister-in-law. Claire went about her allotted chores in a numb trance, transporting potted plants down to the empty hotel, decorating the inner courtyard where the dancing was to be held. The band would be composed of local farmers from the surrounding hills. They brought news that it had been stormy in the mountains behind and the rivers were rising. Manuel was not concerned. There would be indications already, he said, if the weather intended to let them down tonight.

During the morning, needing some extra streamers, Claire drove along the waterfront and into the town. She parked Juanita's car in the square, did her shopping, and was returning when she saw Pascual. She would know that squat figure, that heavy black head, anywhere. He was standing beside Juanita's car, smoking a cigarette. Her first instinct was to turn and run, then she realized that Pascual would be waiting to speak to Juanita, and she came on. As her footsteps echoed across the stone paving the Spaniard looked up.

"*Buenos dias*. I thought you had gone, Señorita," he remarked in surprise.

"I went to get my mother. You know that."

"Ah!" He ground his butt thoughtfully into the stones.

"If you want her, she's at the villa," Claire said pointedly, wanting to get away from him.

Pascual nodded. "I would like to buy you an apéritif, Señorita."

"At this hour?"

"Or *café?*" he replied, shrugging. "I would like to thank you for what has come about for my little girl." He came closer, looking into her face. Now that, for the first time in her dealings with him, there was no threat in his manner, Claire saw an unattractive cockiness in Pascual's gratitude. "You know I have no wife," he said. "There has been no one to care for my little Rosita if I were to die. We lost two children when they were babies, and then my wife died. I am grateful to you, Señorita, for what you have done."

In spite of everything, Claire felt an inrush of sympathy. To a Spaniard this lack of family must indeed be a tragedy. "I understand," she said. "It's kind of you to offer to buy me a drink, but really there's no need." She tried to reach the car door, but Pascual was blocking her way.

"I am a lonely man."

"Yes, I'm sorry. I'm sorry about your daughter, too, Señor Pascual. Truly sorry."

"You're a good girl. A good daughter, Señorita. Juanita will be grateful to you, as I am. Now my little Rosita will be safe in the heart of the Manzales family, if I should die."

So that was it! A family was wanted for Rosita, as well as a husband! Or perhaps the husband did not really matter? Was Ricardo really only Rosita's Club Membership card? Claire bit back her indignation and thought: How quixotic of Fate, to draw upon the enemy!

"You will come and have coffee with me?"

"I'm sorry, Señor Pascual. I'm busy helping with the arrangements for the party. I'll see you tonight."

He looked her up and down. "You're a very beautiful girl, Señorita. There will be many men for you to choose from. Many handsome young men will be at the party."

"Yes," Claire replied mechanically.

"You are so like Juanita whom Ricardo loves. And she is the beautiful mother. Ah!" Pascual hunched his shoulders eloquently, lifted his hands. "Have you seen such photographs as in Manuel's hall?" And without waiting for a reply: "Ricardo, who loves children as every Spaniard loves children, would see you in those pictures. You in your mother's place."

"You realize what you are doing to Ricardo—" She could have bitten her tongue out. She had promised herself there would be no more reproaches.

And Pascual was rough again, cutting her off brusquely. "There will be plenty of nieces and nephews in the Manzales family. Teresa and Leopoldo and the little boys when they grow up, they will all have children. My Rosita will be happy and fulfilled. And so will Ricardo."

Yes, Claire thought, driving back to the hotel with her decorations, it's probably true. Ricardo will still have his family. And, as Juanita had pointed out, he would look elsewhere for his love. It was because of that she had to go. As soon as was decent, she would return to England. She had already told Aunt Marcia to expect her the following week. Uncle Ben had telephoned on receipt of the letter she had sent saying she was, after all, going to help the Manzales family. She had put their minds at peace, if temporarily, but she knew they would not be satisfied until they had her back in England. "Just a brainstorm," she had said wryly on the telephone. A brainstorm! Were they always so painful?

That evening she was to wear her new gold caftan. She looked thoughtfully at the gold shoes Ricardo had given her and wished she had an alternative. Juanita came in looking sweet and feminine in a full-skirted blue gown. "You're lovely, darling. Are you ready? Manuel has the car out."

It was then that panic set in. Claire had thought she was brave. She had thought she was going to be able to carry this off. Suddenly she knew she could not. Her knees were knocking, her hands trembling. Ashen-faced, she said: "I'm sorry,

Juanita. I'm not going to be able to go through with this."

Juanita was upset. Manuel, hearing their distressed voices, crossed the landing. He looked incredibly handsome in his impeccable dinner jacket. He said sternly: "What is this, little Claire? You do not want to come to the party?"

"I'm sorry, Manuel," Claire replied in as calm a voice as she could muster, "but I cannot. I'm very sorry. I simply can't do it."

Manuel turned and strode across the landing. "I will get you a brandy."

But she could not go. She was engulfed, disorientated by the enormity of what was happening. The brandy only made her tearful and lightheaded. It was a fact that she could not, in her present condition, turn up at the party without the possibility of making an exhibition of herself. They left her sitting in her bedroom chair trying, as Juanita urged her, to "pull herself together." As host and hostess, Juanita and Manuel had to be on the party premises before anyone else arrived. From half-way down the stairs Juanita ran back.

"Oh Claire!"

"I'll be all right. I'll come in your car when—if—I feel I can." Claire turned her head away. She did not see the guilty flush on her mother's face, but she knew. Juanita bent down and kissed her. "I'm sorry. I'd do anything—"

Claire looked around, her eyes tortured with the agony in her. "Would you? Would you do anything for me?"

Manuel called brusquely from downstairs: "Juanita, we are late." Without a word, her mother left.

EIGHTEEN

Hours passed. Claire had not even risen to turn on the light. Suddenly there was a soft pattering on the vine leaves outside her window. Rain? She dragged herself stiffly to her feet and looked out. The air was cool and very still. Surely rain would bring disaster to the party, for they would not be able to continue dancing in the courtyard where there was no shelter except for one small eucalyptus tree which had been carefully preserved during the building. The gaily clothed little chairs and tables were set in the courtyard too. The rain was growing heavier by the moment. Claire's mind jumped ahead. Such rain could break up a gathering and send everyone home. What if they all came back here? She felt unnerved at the thought of facing them. Could she escape?

Almost before she had come to a decision she

began sliding out of her gold caftan. She unbuckled her shoes and kicked them off, then pulled on a pair of jeans, a sweater and a pair of walking shoes. Flinging a waterproof jacket around herself, she sped down the stairs, picked up Juanita's car keys and ran out to the garage. The rain was falling heavily now. She started the engine and drove out of the drive, down the hill, along the coast road, and skirting the town turned up into the hills. Now that she was free, now there was no possibility of meeting anyone, she breathed a sigh of relief then immediately had to take stock of her situation for at that moment it seemed the heavens opened. Inevitably, she braked. If this kept on she would have to stop, for even in spite of the whirring windscreen wipers she could scarcely see. Where was she? There were two roads going in this direction from the town. One should lead to Manuel's *finca*, and the other should turn into the hills farther north. There was no knowing which one she had taken for the rain obliterated all landmarks. Even if she had, by chance, taken the road to the *finca*, would she find it in this downpour?

The gradient was steep here. Already the road was awash for the rain was cascading down from the heights above and there were no gutters or drains to carry it away. Too late she realized she was running into the heart of a very severe storm. She would have turned and raced back down the hill but there was nowhere wide enough to turn. Suddenly a flash of lightning lit up the whole landscape, and immediately a deafening blast of thunder echoed frighteningly around and around the hills. Unable to see through the windscreen,

Claire pulled over to the bank and switched the engine off, leaving the lights on. Dirty yellow flood water poured down the road and swirled around the car. Nervously, she checked the handbrake. If the situation worsened, this tiny Fiat had no hope of holding the road. There was another flash of lightning and in its light she saw, terrifyingly, the bank above over which water was cascading in a crazy, billowing curtain. The ensuing clap of thunder shot Claire half out of her seat and nearly deafened her. Where was all this water coming from? And then she realized that these barren, often almost perpendicular rocky hills had little soil to act as catchment for the rain. With a tremor of raw fear she remembered there was little enough soil even to hold the stones that were everywhere. As though the thought had come as a warning, hurly burly over the bank came a rush of small boulders, their impetus carrying them across the road and down into the valley below. Claire scrabbled in the glove compartment for a flashlight but there was none. What to do? Risk being trapped in a car as it hurtled down the hillside? Or jump out and take a chance on avoiding the stones? There was an earsplitting crack. The car rocked as it was hit by a boulder and then a shower of smaller stones. Claire screamed, fumbled frantically with the door catch, realized she was on the wrong side, took a clumsy sideways leap to the passenger seat and fell out into the road, not knowing what to do or where to run. Water streamed around her legs, tugging at her jeans. Water streamed through her hair and down her face so that she could not see. In a panic, she ran forward, then back. The next time the lightning came it lit up the sky to the east and the thunder rolled more distantly. Miraculously, the storm was moving on. At the same time the rain eased a little and Claire felt the panic subsiding.

She hurried around the car to survey the damage. The boulder that had hit her was enormous. It had struck the rear wheel, shifting the car into a forty-five degree turn. She went back down the road to see if, in the event of her being able to get the car around, she was going to be able to use the road.

The landslide was less than a hundred yards behind, a great pile of stones, mud and debris. Though her eyes were growing accustomed to the darkness, Claire could not see the full extent of the damage nor how far the landslide stretched down the hillside. But she could see there was to be no returning. The car would have to be abandoned. She must start walking before the family began to worry about her. Hugging her wet jacket round her, she felt her way tentatively over the dripping bank below the road. There was plenty of undergrowth for footholds and plenty of tough little bushes for handholds. She inched her way down the steep slope, keeping close to the edge of the landslide so that she would not lose her way.

It was not far to the bottom, perhaps a hundred yards or so. Claire breathed a sigh of relief as she came to what looked like the end of the debris. She felt her way forwards through waist-high scrub and bracken, then began the climb.

Suddenly, to her surprise, she heard voices. She paused, listening. Yes. They were men's voices. She opened her mouth to call out, then hesitated. She was, after all, alone on a dark hillside in a strange country. She did not speak the language. And she had no idea where she was. She climbed slowly up the hill, picking her way through the wet scrub, not daring to turn aside in case she should lose herself. When she neared the road she could move at right angles to it until she was out of sight and earshot, then climb the rest of the way. She went from handhold to handhold. Above there was an argument in progress. One of the men swore. Even in Spanish, Claire could recognize an oath, delivered as it was with such intensity. Frightened, she was turning right to cross the hillside when there was the crack of a branch and then a woman's scream. Claire's blood froze.

Then Ricardo's voice—she would know that voice anywhere—said in English: "May God forgive you, Fernando, for this."

Claire leaped to her feet. "Ricardo! Ricardo, it's me. Claire."

"Claire!" he shouted. "My God, Claire, what are you doing here? Where are you?"

"I'm here." She blundered upwards through the undergrowth, scrabbling on hands and knees, slipping, falling, almost sobbing with excitement. She could see Ricardo now, a dark form standing at the roadside waiting for her. He held out both arms and she grasped his hands. He pulled her up the bank on to the road. "What on earth. . . ?"

"I was driving. I didn't want to go to the party. I took Juanita's car. It's stuck on the other side of this slide."

"Humph," said Pascual's voice. "The English girl."

She peered through the darkness towards him. "I heard a woman scream."

Ricardo said: "Perhaps you would talk to Rosita. Her father wants to carry her around this pile. He's already tried to go through but it's a bog."

"Carry her?" echoed Claire. "But he can't. It's quite steep in parts." She went towards the car. The door was open and Pascual sat on the seat with the girl in his lap. She was wearing a long-skirted dress with a cloak over the top. She said querulously: "You climbed around. My father is very strong."

Pascual rose and holding his daughter in his arms, walked to the edge of the road. Ricardo said angrily, "You're drunk, Fernando. For God's sake, put Rosita back in the car." When Pascual ignored him, he said, "Rosita, this is madness."

She spoke to him provocatively in Spanish and he replied, still angry: "I would never do it. I cannot do it any more than your father can. The ground is too steep, and too slippery. I will not be responsible."

"If you will not, then my father must do it," she replied, using the voice of a spoiled child. Pascual was already moving over the edge of the bank.

"Put her down," shouted Ricardo, and Pascual said thickly: "Don't touch me. Don't touch me, or I may drop her, and you will be to blame."

They stood there helplessly while the Spaniard with the girl in his arms went down the steep little bank. He was indeed sure-footed. Claire said in a low voice: "He may do it. He may manage. He must be as strong as an ox."

"And what if it rains again? Rosita will be soaked to the skin.'

Even as he spoke, rain began to fall, softly at first and then insistently. Ricardo called to Pascual in Spanish but there was no reply.

"Why didn't he take her to Manuel's villa?" Claire asked, distressed.

"He had a fight with Manuel. He was drinking too much, and boasting. Manuel put him down and he turned nasty. It's no good arguing with him," Ricardo said despairingly. "It only makes things worse. The man's mad." Rain was falling heavily now. They could hear Rosita whimpering.

"Where do they live?"

"Not far from here."

"There's my car."

"Yes, I was thinking of that. I'm going to go after them."

Ricardo leaped down the bank and Claire followed him. Pascual and the girl were making good progress. She could see Pascual's dark form not far ahead. He must be as sure-footed as a mountain goat. The rain seemed to spur him on and indeed he did not slide or slip as Claire was doing. They reached the bottom of the slide and turned. The going was faster here on the level ground. Then, on the edge of the landslide, Pascual stopped. In the murky darkness Claire could see that the ground here rose steeply, too steeply for Pascual to climb with the burden of his daughter in his arms. Below, the hillside fell away into scree. Without realizing it, they had come upon a narrow track which Claire had missed on her way over by going farther down the hillside to avoid the patch of scree now directly beneath him.

Ricardo said: "You'll have to keep going straight ahead until there's an easier slope. Let me take her, Fernando. You go on and find a better track."

Pascual, breathing heavily, made no reply. He had turned his head towards the precipitate rise and as though Ricardo had not spoken, was deliberating on its climbability.

Ricardo said shortly: "Let me go in front, then," and made to push past. Pascual said something in Spanish and Ricardo gave a cry of protest. He held out his arms, then when Fernando did not move, let them fall to his sides. Rosita began complaining in Spanish, then she too was silent. The rain was falling steadily.

Ricardo stepped back a little way along the track towards Claire, throwing his bitter remark over his shoulder: "I should have thought this downpour would have sobered you up, you damned lunatic." Then: "Are you all right, Rosita?"

"No," replied the girl. She was shivering uncontrollably, and she sounded frightened.

Ricardo said, speaking calmly and carefully: "If you'd only allow me to pass, I could find you a reasonable track. Couldn't you move ahead? I don't dare push in case I knock you off balance."

Pascual ignored him. Still breathing heavily, he seemed to be taking measure of the steep slope. Almost as though, perversely, he would risk disaster rather than accept help from the younger man. Then slowly, testing each foothold, snatching at a bush with his left hand to redress his balance, he began to move up the perilous slope with the girl in his arms.

Ricardo gasped, swore under his breath, then moved in behind. "Keep clear," he barked at Claire. "They haven't a hope . . ." The warning remained unfinished. There was a rattle of falling stones, a crack as a branch or root broke and suddenly Pascual overbalanced. Ricardo gave a cry and what seemed like a black swirl of bodies came tumbling past. Claire screamed, then suddenly she was sliding and slipping too, over the track and down the rocky face.

There was not far to go. Perhaps fifteen feet, and then their fall was broken by some heavy undergrowth bolstered by what must have been thin saplings. They struggled to extricate themselves from each other, to stand upright.

"Rosita!" Claire exclaimed. "Rosita! Are you all right?" Ricardo also was calling her name and then Pascual.

"Rosita!"

"Rosita!"

"Rosita!"

Their frightend voices gave way to the noise of the rain spattering on leaves. Pascual began to jabber hysterically in Spanish. Ricardo said in a barely controlled voice through which the alarm rang clear: "Keep still, Fernando. She's got to be here close by. Move carefully."

"What's happened to her?" Claire found herself asking the useless question out loud. "She must have fallen further, Ricardo. She must have slipped past the bushes." They thrashed around in the wet undergrowth. The saplings that had broken their fall seemed to stand in a line, close together. Claire said in a puzzled voice: "She can't have fallen any farther. There's no way." And then, with infinite relief: "She's got to be above us! She must be lying where her father dropped her." She lifted her head. "Rosita! Rosita! Are you there?"

Through the listening silence there came the shuffle of wet leaves, the crack of a twig, and Claire cried in delight: "She's okay. She didn't fall!" They leaped forward together, and together made the track. Claire scrabbled up the steeply rising bank from which Pascual had slipped, reached another path and then paused, bewildered. "She isn't here!" In a strange sort of eerie panic she found herself screaming: "Rosita!"

And then, from high above came a petulant voice, speaking in Spanish. For one crazy moment Claire thought some other woman had come down from the road and she cried: "Stop! There's been an accident."

Rosita said querulously: "You ask *me* to stop! Who is hurt? My father? Can't you attend to him?"

It seemed than that none of them could either speak or move. They stood in the steady rain like three people turned to stone while the rustling in the bushes above grew fainter. Then Ricardo said in a queer, shaken voice with something like strained laughter showing through: "Perhaps you knew she could walk, Fernando, huh?"

Pascual took off like a rocket, floundering up the steep bank, sliding and slipping back, grasping ferociously at hand holds, grunting. There was something about his haste that triggered off alarm

in Claire's mind, and at the same moment Ricardo
leaped after him. "Fernando!"

Though Pascual had a start he was older,
heavier and a good deal less agile than either
Ricardo or Claire. They caught him up a yard
short of the road. His breathing was coming in
short, angry gasps. The rain had lessened. There
was no sign of Rosita but with their eyes
accustomed to the darkness they could see the
outline of the car. They ran towards it and there
was the girl seated on the front seat with her legs in
the road and the door wide. Pascual lumbered
across the intervening space, breathing heavily,
then before Ricardo could stop him lifted his right
hand and swung it in an outraged, stinging slap
across his daughter's cheek. Rosita, screaming,
fell back against the upholstery and Ricardo
swung Pascual around in a deadly spin that threw
him off balance so that he fell in the road. "You
had better walk," said Ricardo coldly. "I'm going
to get Rosita home." Then, turning to the girl
asked: "Are you all right, Rosita?"

"No," replied Pascual's daughter, shaking
uncontrollably. Ricardo helped her gently into
the back seat.

The keys were in the dash for Claire had
forgotten to remove them. Claire and Ricardo slid
into the front seat without another word.
Thankfully, the engine started, but as Ricardo put
his foot on the accelerator and released the brake
there was an appalling crunching of metal.
Ricardo swore.

"It's the boulder. It was hit by a boulder,"
Claire explained.

They jumped out and put their combined

weight against the boulder, managed to rock it out
of position. "You get back in and move the car."
Claire slid into the driving seat, started the engine,
put the car into gear and freed it. She turned as she
slipped back to the passenger seat. She was
worried by Rosita's silence. She could hear her
shivering now, the chattering of her teeth. Pascual
had disappeared in the darkness. They did not
speak again. The tiny car was laboring with its
heavy load. Some distance along the road they
turned up a steep drive. Lights sprang out of the
darkness.

They pulled in by a white-painted overhang.
Ricardo leaped out and helped Rosita from the
car. He banged the knocker on the door. Two old
women came. For the first time, in the light from
the terrace, Claire saw Rosita's face, marble white
within its frame of wet black hair, the head held
arrogantly high but the eyes turned away. One of
the women gave a shriek of excitement. Ricardo
spoke brusquely and they all went inside. Claire
turned. This was no place for her. She went back
to the car, her mind in a turmoil.

It must have been ten minutes later that Pascual
lumbered by and without turning his head went
straight into the house. A few minutes passed then
Ricardo emerged. He was clearly disturbed but he
seemed to have his emotions in control. Climbing
into the driving seat, he said: "I've called the
doctor. He's on his way. We will pick him up at
the landslide." He started the car, then turned, a
bleak smile on his face, and put a warm hand over
her cold one.

"Look, I think you'd better go into the house
and wait. We can't trust the brakes now. That

torrent running down the road will almost certainly have got into the brake linings. And the road is slippery as ice. But I must meet the doctor."

"No. I want to come with you."

"Then keep your hand on the door, and your fingers crossed."

They drove carefully down the road. Because she did not want to talk about Rosita's duplicity, Claire volunteered: "Miranda Cervera said Pascual wouldn't be content to get his own way. That he enjoys feuding with the Manzales."

"Did she?" Ricardo shook himself out of some sort of trance to show grim amusement. "Well, she was right. Only how can I get that across to Manuel? Manuel believes there's an angel in everyone if you give it a chance to appear. But there isn't. You've seen that tonight. There's a devil in Fernando Pascual and it's never going to die. What's in his daughter?" He turned to Claire, looking quizzical. "You should know more about women than I."

She reached across and touched his hand tenderly. "I don't seem to know much about anything. I can't even believe what has happened."

He said grimly: "It's not easy to imagine anyone padding around her bedroom when everyone's back is turned. But she must have done a good bit of it to have the strength to climb that hill."

Claire did not want to talk about Rosita's outrageous behavior because it might mean having to face the possibility that a very real love could drive her to such lengths. She wanted to hold onto sympathy because Rosita, whatever she had done, was frail and perhaps badly chilled. Who knew what might happen after such an experience? Whatever exercise she had taken secretly, in the privacy of her own room, she had certainly not faced the elements for a long time. "Tell me what happened to bring you here," she said.

"Back at the party? Fernando, after getting annoyed with Manuel, picked up Rosita and simply carried her off. I was afraid he wasn't capable of driving in the state he was in so I tried to get behind the wheel, but Rosita was excited. She started shrieking and I was afraid for her—" He broke off.

"Go on," said Claire gently.

Ricardo seemed to shake himself out of some sort of trance. "I followed them in my car, just in case something went wrong. If I had known Fernando was going to do that stupid thing I'd have knocked him flat before he got hold of Rosita, but by the time I realized what I was up against he had Rosita in his arms, and it was too late. He was like a madman with a hostage. And Rosita didn't help. She's so used to people doing things for her that she—" He broke off again.

They arrived at the landslide and Claire climbed out. The rain seemed to be over. Even the small torrent that had been running down from the hills had eased considerably. She helped Ricardo turn the car round in the narrow road, backing and filling, backing and filling, until at last it had gone safely full circle. They sat close together in the front seat, arms around each other, trying to keep warm, until they heard the engine of the doctor's car. Ricardo climbed out. He shouted instructions in Spanish across the pile of debris. Claire climbed into the back seat. She was soaked to the skin and her teeth were chattering with cold. It seemed an age before the doctor arrived, wet and gasping for breath. If he knew she was there he took no notice. As they drove back up the hill the two men talked in Spanish. The doctor seemed at once angry and grimly amused.

As he went through the front door of the villa Ricardo turned with a gesture of concern. "You're frozen. Get into the front with me. My God, you're soaked!" He held her tightly against him, and she knew immediately that it had less to do with the fact that she was cold than because he really needed her. He seemed to be in a state of shock.

"There's something I have to say," she began. "I know you better than you think. You're going to want to unravel all this gently. I'd like to disappear while you do it. Don't say you need me. Not now. You're very strong. You've coped all the way to date. I want to be able to feel you're content with the winding up. Rosita may—" She swallowed, remembering how urgently the doctor had been summoned. "That was an immense effort for a girl who has spent so many months in bed, or a chair. And she must be so wet. Miranda Cervera has issued me with an open invitation. I'd like to go tomorrow."

"All right," he replied, "but let me say something. I want you to know that that day I gave in to Rosita's hysterics and allowed her to ride pillion I said to myself: 'This is the last time, the very last time that she and I do anything together.'" He added with that sweet smile of his: "She was fun, for a while."

For the fun he had paid dearly. "Because he is a gentleman," Teresa said later.

Everyone agreed that Claire should go back to Tangier for a while. The Manzales family had, incongruously, taken Fernando Pascual in his penitence and embarrassment to their vast, warm bosom once again. That his love would not last was a foregone conclusion but for the moment the same warm sun shone over them all.

"They're good on forgiveness," said Miranda Cervera, smiling, "just as they're good at taking and giving. Poor Pascual. That dreadful girl made a proper fool of him. Well, she's survived. I had a letter from Juanita this morning. Rosita comes out of the hospital tomorrow. You knew she contracted pneumonia?"

"No," replied Claire, startled.

"No, of course not," Miranda replied placidly, avoiding her eyes. "I forgot to tell you." Miranda's American husband had returned. The house in the medina was gay with his western presence, his lively laughter. "As you would say, he is like a bull in a china shop, but he enjoys Tangier. Only because he can get back to New York any time he wants to, of course."

They took Claire to the belly dancing and the bazaars. They escorted her over the Sultan's Palace and dined her on exotic food in dark restaurants where fat waiters wearing the red fez waited on her every whim. They drove her to the Atlas Mountains from which she gazed in awe over the vast expanse of arid hills and sandy plains that was the beginning of the African desert. They calmed her and taught her patience.

And then Ricardo came. He arrived unannounced in the middle of the morning when Miranda was supervising the housework and her husband had gone off into the town. Claire was crossing the court when he came through the vine-hung entrance. His gleaming black hair lay across his broad forehead in luxuriant waves and his eyes within those thick, spiky lashes were such an incredible blue. It was like slipping back in time to the day Claire had first seen him crossing the little square in front of the church after Luiz the barman telephoned to say Señora Manzales's daughter had arrived. She had that strange sensation again, as of sliding through to her destiny, only this time there was no surprise. Neither of them spoke a word. They moved together and before the interested gaze of a clutch of black-eyed, long-gowned servants, Ricardo's arms enfolded her.

"Are you ready?" he asked. "I want to take you home."

He told them the great news as they ate lunch in the palmfilled, ornately decorated diningroom. That his plans for the new hospital had been accepted and that Manuel, after an inevitable, initial explosion, had wished him luck. There was an exciting, busy, wonderful time ahead. Floyd Cervera, on hearing the news, insisted on bringing out the champagne and they drank to the success of the great venture.

"There will be time to get married," Ricardo said, "but no time for a honeymoon now."

Claire sat up, startled. "Is that a public proposal?"

He only held her hand tightly and replied with confidence: "You've always known it had to be."

Spontaneously, she leaned across to kiss him. "There was a time when you could have fooled me. Well, since we're getting married, I'd like my English relations to come."

Ricardo said drolly: "Did I forget to tell you? They're here, with swords bared. Juanita has taken them in."

"The things you forget!" Claire was delighted. "They looked after me a good deal of the time. How nice of them to be so unnecessarily concerned." They raised their glasses and drank to Marcia, Nancy and Ben.

Claire and Ricardo caught the afternoon ferry. They had no need of the scudding, busy, noisy little hydrofoil, for the rest of the day was theirs. They stood close together in the bow with arms entwined and a fresh Mediterranean breeze in their faces. The brown hills of Africa crept away behind and the grand, old, lion-like Rock of Gibraltar welcomed them benevolently in.

"Do you think we could do up the house at the *finca?*" Claire asked.

He gave her a shrewd look. "Meaning?"

"You love it."

"And?"

"All right, if I must say it out loud. Manuel takes his lady friends there."

"Don't try to change Manuel, darling," Ricardo said. "Juanita knows, and loves, her man. He is what he is. And if he is a despot, he is a truly benevolent one. Those who must, slide out from under. You saw me do it. Of course I'd love to do up that old house and live there. Let's wait and see which way the wind blows, shall we? I couldn't afford it at the moment, anyway. You're marrying a poor man. You know that, don't you?"

Claire gave him a puzzled, amused, sideways look. "I'm never sure." As the sun went down over Cape St Vincent way, the ferry boat crept into Algeciras. Claire said: "What happened to the ring?"

Ricardo put a hand in his pocket and drew out a box. An enormous emerald lay on a velvet pad. Claire blinked, stared, and blinked again.

Ricardo's eyes twinkled. "You're thinking of the Wishing Ring. It's gone back to Josefina. Your mother did give it to Rosita but she didn't want to wish." Odd, how naturally they talked about Rosita.

"Did you buy this, or is it part of your family treasure trove?" Claire asked in astonishment as Ricardo slipped the lovely ring on her finger. "For a family who reckons itself poor, you have some astonishing assets."

He put an arm around her shoulders and looked affectionately down into her face.

"We have assets indeed."

ROMANTIC SUSPENSE

Discover ACE's exciting new line of exotic romantic suspense novels by award-winning author Anne Worboys:

THE LION OF DELOS

RENDEZVOUS WITH FEAR

THE WAY OF THE TAMARISK

THE BARRANCOURT DESTINY

Coming soon:

HIGH HOSTAGE